T0088897

I AM HER

CASSANDRA CILLITTO

BALBOA.PRESS

A DIVISION OF HAY HOUSE

Balboa Press books may be ordered through booksellers or by contacting:

Balboa Press
A Division of Hay House
1663 Liberty Drive
Bloomington, IN 47403
www.balboapress.com
844-682-1282

Because of the dynamic nature of the Internet, any web addresses or
links contained in this book may have changed since publication and
may no longer be valid. The views expressed in this work are solely those
of the author and do not necessarily reflect the views of the publisher,
and the publisher hereby disclaims any responsibility for them.

The author of this book does not dispense medical advice or prescribe
the use of any technique as a form of treatment for physical, emotional,
or medical problems without the advice of a physician, either directly
or indirectly. The intent of the author is only to offer information
of a general nature to help you in your quest for emotional and
spiritual well-being. In the event you use any of the information in
this book for yourself, which is your constitutional right, the author
and the publisher assume no responsibility for your actions.

Any people depicted in stock imagery provided by Getty Images are
models, and such images are being used for illustrative purposes only.
Certain stock imagery © Getty Images.

Print information available on the last page.

ISBN: 978-1-9822-5551-0 (sc)
ISBN: 978-1-9822-5552-7 (e)

Balboa Press rev. date: 09/25/2020

Thank you to my husband for giving me the time to create this and to my kids for always believing in me. Thank you to Keir for setting it in motion.

Contents

Meet and Greet

What a beautiful day, cloudy with a chance of more clouds, just a typical day in good old Half Moon Bay. Since I can remember it has been the same here, sixty five degrees and overcast, that's what makes it okay. It is quiet and you know what to expect. The weather never changes. I remember waking up for the first day of school in second grade ready to wear my new outfit; a cute cotton t-shirt dress but it was raining out so my Mom made me put on a raincoat that covered my new clothes. Sadly I thought shopping was pointless after that. No need to make an impression. Jeans and a t-shirt are a quality go to staple in Half Moon Bay and I wasn't going to catch any ones attention anyway.

I am plain as plain can be. Sarah Plain and Tall if you will. I am average per every scale. Brown hair and light olive skin, able to blend in with most races, no features to set me apart; that is Me. My neighbors would forget who I was if I hadn't lived here my whole life. Sadly I think most forget who I am and or are surprised I am still around. I am in good shape but not overly muscular, still very feminine. I train 6 days a week and it keeps me in tip-top physical health. I think I look good in a bikini. I am average height. I bet you knew a girl like me growing up. I always remind people of someone they know or have met before. Someone they remember but can not remember their name. I am easily forgotten. I would like to think I have a good personality but I do not stand out so people tend to overlook me. Though as a young middle school girl this used to make me cry when the popular boys never noticed me but as an adult is something that I have come to terms with and find very helpful in my line of work.

Half Moon Bay is a small town feel though it has grown and grown over the years. When I was young we all played out in the street until the streetlights went on. Now its like no one comes out to socialize anymore.

I live in my childhood home. My dad sold me my own home about three years ago after my mom died. I had been living in the city. I had a fun little flat near little Italy. It was an expensive little tin box but was closed to good food and I loved the people watching. Felt like I was living the dream. Though I loved being in the heart of San Francisco I thought why not…. I'll go back to the same place I originally became invisible. My house is pretty much the same though I have updated the kitchen and it has a fresh coat of paint inside and out, but the biggest improvement was done to what I call the dungeon. Dad was not happy I changed the dungeon but it is mine now. I spend a great deal of time down there so I had to make it my own. I had to make it comfortable.

I miss the city from time to time. The city was a fun place. I could be apart of the action without having to know anyone. Remember I blend in. But now that I have made the dungeon mine, I am okay with not being out and about all the time. Sounds kind of lonely and pathetic but that is my life. The dungeon is a place I usually get lost in. It is like a casino; I go in and lose all track of time. It is my sanctuary; a place I can truly be me. I love to fiddle with my weapons and gadgets and get lost in my research.

I work in the city still so there is that. I have a small office in an old brick building off Market Street. I am by appointment only so I never have visitors. I go into the office to maintain appearances. I have a small waiting room, looks bigger than it is because of the huge window that overlooks the city. The natural light gives it an airy feel. Never would anyone feel unsafe here. My office is nice. Nothing fancy but everything is modern and clean. One would think I have a small space. Being that my dad has owned the building for the last 20 years, I can get away with having extra 1000 square feet of hidden space behind my desk wall. Thanks to dad it is already filled with every weapon imaginable, a workout space, a full kitchen and bathroom. Being that I took over the family business it is all mine now, nothing like going to work to sharpen knives and clean firearms.

Just to clarify I am not a total loner or weirdo. I do have one really good friend. Her name is Danielle. Danielle and I meet at Deborah's Birthday sleepover in the first grade and have been best friends ever since. We bonded over the movie Aladdin. The intro to the movie had us laughing all night. So lame but we have been friends ever since. We grew up in different neighborhoods but went to the same school. I'm from a more blue collard area where her family had the big two-story house off Kelly. She is exotic looking. Italian and Lebanese. She has strong features, dark curly hair and a big personality. I guess it is why we are perfect friends. She has a big heart like me. We want to help everyone. We give people the benefit of the doubt. Though she is outspoken and verbally passionate. I am quiet and accomplish my goals quietly through other means. If we were a concert she would be the performer and I would be the behind the scenes manager.

Danielle was the athlete super star and I was more of the geek. My hobbies included problem solving and learning to fight. Yep, learning to fight. Being one of three girls my dad made us all learn Karate. Karate is a general term. We actually all learned Capoeria, Jeet Kune Doand Hung Ga. Though I took it to the next level and learned all the weapons. I can really kick some ass. It is a good stress reliever. I might be a ghost but a ghost that could kill you. Capoeria was my favorite to learn. It is an Afro-Brazillian martial art that kind of looks like a dance. I think it was my favorite because I was not one of the dance girls and it made me feel connected somehow. It has helped me with my power, speed and leverage in out maneuvering my opponents.

My dad made us, all learn how to use a gun. My older sister took it as important knowledge to apply to life but my younger sister thought it was dreadful. The first time she chipped a nail loading my dads Springfield XD 40 she complained for weeks. It is a bitch to load past ten but I think my dad was using it as a lesson. Each gun is different but for the most part guns have been streamlined. I really think he was testing our personalities. It wasn't long after this he started taking me out shooting without my sisters.

They got to the point where my dad was satisfied with their knowledge but for some reason, may be my added interest, he taught me more and more. My shooting starter pack consisted of a .22 Caliber, 38 Special, and a Colt Dragoon Revolver. This was after my basic BB Gun training. The fundamentals of shooting out the dots on print outs can be applied across the board. I think my dad was going through an old west movie marathon obsession back then but I learned how to load, unload, disarm and hit my targets. I also had to clean all of them before I was allowed to 'advance' as my dad would call it.

While Danielle was playing volleyball and softball I was learning gun safety, accurizing, how to make black powder, how to use a bore snake, and how to zero-in. Dad took it upon himself to teach me to be a skilled sniper before I graduated High School. I guess that is why he never worried about me going out with my friends because he knew my lethal potential. Not that he needed to worry; Half Moon Bay wasn't that happening and I was never invited to stuff anyway.

I didn't attend Half Moon Bay High School like Danielle. My sisters and I attended Notre Dame, the all girls Catholic College Prep high school in Belmonte, or as we say, over the hill. I had to wake up forty-five minuets earlier than most just to get to school on time. The 92 in the morning could be okay or bumper-to-bumper. One lane in and one lane out made the morning commute so much fun. The nice thing about going to High School with my sisters was I didn't have to socialize much. My older sister graduated after my freshman year and I was only a loner my sophomore year because my younger sister was a freshman my junior year. Oddly that is when High School got interesting. She was and is still is as social as they come. I was invited to everything because my dad would not let her go alone. Most of the time I could just find a corner and hide. I started to study people at these parties. Really seeing people for who they are. The jocks and preps from Serra, the desperation of young people kept people watching interesting. The mix of the Carlmont public school kids always made for a fun night. My sister always had someone to talk to and would move around the room with ease. I swear she could have become a politician.

My Past

I t was at one of these parties that I first witnessed something that got my blood to boil and changed me forever. There was an older guy there. No one really knew how old he was. Sad he was at a High School party, I wasn't the biggest loser there apparently. Even though he stuck out and obviously should not have been there no one said anything to him or asked him to leave. If someone had just asked him to leave it could have changed the course of my life.

He made his way over to one of my sisters friends. He wouldn't take no for an answer. She was not having it at first, but he didn't give up. She was cute and totally not aware of her body. I think her name was Jill. She had no clue how pretty she was. When she originally dissed him, his body language changed. Instead of becoming angry and aggressive he became soft, caring, and flirty. He got her a drink, then another one, and then another one. I just sat in my dark corner memorized by his performance. He knew exactly what he was doing. He had a plan, a mission and I was going to keep an eye on him.

He touched her hair, wrapped it around her finger. Laughed at what she was saying. I don't think he had a clue what she was talking about but it didn't matter. He appeared to be one hundred percent into her and she was eating it up. Jill actually warmed up to him. He touched her arm. She giggled. It got to the point when they got up because she had to pee. He helped her to the bathroom upstairs of this house party we were at. He went inside even though she clearly was uncomfortable with it.

I waited a minuet and decided to investigate. I felt something was wrong and followed my gut. Something was off about the whole interaction. He was there with a purpose, not someone that just wanted to hang on a Friday night. I was stunned no one saw what happened or notice she left with him. Where my peers that clueless? The door was locked so I put my ear to the door to listen. It sounded like there was heavy lifting going on with a hint of aggravation. It didn't sound right. For the first time I felt something was wrong so I used one of my hairpins to pick the lock. What I saw when I opened the door was a horror I never imagined. In that second I changed as a person, I changed as a human and I acted on instinct.

The next day and the following week there was not a word of what happened at the party. It was like it didn't happen. I had to play it over and over again in my mind to make sure it was real. Was I that invisible that no one had seen what I did? What he did? The aftermath? The experience had me in a trance. I felt like I wasn't even present in anything I did. I would drive to my destination and not remember how I got there.

A week had pasted when my dad approached me. Apparently I was still sitting in my car from the ride home from school an hour after getting home, engine off and staring into space. Dad knew what had happened. I had called him after what I did. I wasn't scared but for once was at a loss of what my next course of action was. It was automatic and no emotion attached to it. Dad calmly gave my bullet point instructions and hung up the phone. He went to pick up my sister from the party telling her I got ill and went home earlier in the night.

When I got home and showered I noticed my dirty clothes were gone. I never saw them again after that. Jill didn't come to school that following week. I checked the office records that following Friday. She had fallen "ill" and was getting her work sent home until she made a full recovery. It was easy to slip into the office and find out all the information on anyone I wanted. No one ever seemed to notice me. Then and there I was aware of myself and what I was able to do.

Dad came to my truck window and just looked at me. Nodded and I followed him inside.

I was supposed to go to some movie with Danielle that night but my dad told her I was still not feeling well. Something was always going around. With my mom visiting my older sister at Cal Poly San Louis Obispo and my little sister at cheer practice, it gave dad a chance to introduce me to the family business.

Until that afternoon I thought my dad was the CEO of a Marketing Firm in the City. Mom was the secretary and youth director of Our Lady of the Pillar Catholic Church. Dad however traveled a lot. Always trying to secure that one big account. We were never hurt for money. While my mom pressed us on the importance of the Catholic Faith, church every Sunday, C.C.D., youth group, Dad always preached being kind. His philosophy was to do to others, as you wanted done to you; simple but effective. He wanted us to be kind and try and see the good in everyone. He was a retired Marine. He never talked about what he saw during his service but I think it stayed with him. He always said there was an evil out there. Something we could never change, but we could make a difference.

Today was the day when I learned what difference I could make. We walked inside the house and mid way down the hall my dad made a motion. For once I was not paying one hundred percent attention to my surroundings. With that the floor in front of us started to move. The floor opened up and lead me into the dungeon. I named it the dungeon for a couple reasons. It is creepy and I never knew it was under our house. Like most homes on the cost there had been bomb shelters in the back yards. Some of my friends even had basements though it is more of a Midwest thing.

Walking down into the dungeon my dad flipped the lights on. It was warm lighting. Like something you would have in a study or library. Enough to see clearly but nothing you could examine computer parts with. While in the dungeon my eyes darted all over the walls. There was not one spot that was not covered in weaponry. I knew why dad was a collector but this was next level. Remember, I was a junior in high school that just committed a crime to save a girl and my dad is taking me into a secret room that has enough gadgets to kill millions.

To clarify what happens next is most important to me. So you understand, growing up Catholic is one thing, being hammered the catholic rules and one must do this and that is a lot. Are we allowed to make mistakes? I was always on the fence about how are people supposed to live and learn? My biggest hang up has always been the true evils of the world: the evils that are the murderers and rapist, the ones whom hurt for pleasure, the ones who hurt children especially. It is something that I have not been able to move past. May be that is why the conversation with my father went so well. I just can't imagine a Heaven filled with these evil people of the world because Jesus sacrificed himself for our sins. So its like "No worries, no matter what your in!"

I always thought Jesus sacrificed himself so we could make the mistakes, learn from our actions, repent, live and learn. Not: "Sally, Welcome your rapist that butchered you when you were ten into Heaven. Aren't you glad to have him join us?"

Once not long ago I had a conversation with an old friend about this. Bridget truly believes everyone goes to Heaven. There is no Hell. So is Hell on Earth? The sicko's that enjoy harming children get a free pass just because? I really do not know what to believe, but I do know that in a weird way what I do know helps me cope with that. I may be killing people but I only kill the bad ones. Like a female Robin Hood type. I may be justifying because two wrongs do not make a right but I really only go after the bad ones.

From this point on I started on my path to justice. I know God will judge me in the end but I finally had a purpose: A passion, something that I have continued to excel at and it almost seems like I was made for it.

My family comes from a long line of protectors, people whom have fought to protect others: The right to the wrong; on a quest to rid the world of its true evils. There have been generations that have passed on the training. Some generations with multiple family members involved. What happened at the party was no accident. It was a wake up call to what I was meant to do and who I have been all along. I was going to protect those around me. Even if they didn't know I was there. I had been floating through life. Now I had a goal and a mission. Something I truly believed in. My invisibility was no longer a social nightmare but my secret weapon.

After hours of questions and answers my dad sent me to my room. The next day I started my training. I was officially and Intern for my dads marketing company. My mom was so happy I had an after school activity to do. Apparently I read too much. I would meet dad afterschool and we would go over scouting, exit planning, observing our surroundings. He made me memorize the Bart schedule, sporting schedules, special events. I had an intense weapon training twice a week along with three combat classes. As bad as it may seem I had purpose and no matter what it was I was finally thankful to have a focus, something that I was apart of.

Super Bowl came around well into my training and while most of my friend's barbequed and hung out, I got to go on my first assignment. I made two kills that night.

No one saw me and I left no evidence, being invisible has its advantages. That night I became aware of how much I liked using a knife and why my dad had me run so many laps.

Everyday Encounters

ack to the present, another day in Half Moon Bay. I am supposed to meet Danielle at Meza Luna for dinner. She has some big news to tell me. I have a feeling Matt finally purposed. Danielle and Matt have been dating since high school. Though they have never been with anyone else they are the type that will be together forever. They work. College was hard on them but now that they both have good jobs I think he finally made the move. For some reason I always thought she would be the one to ask him, apparently he has balls after all.

My drive to the city is uneventful. I drive a Ford Mustang. Nothing fancy but it is fun to drive. I try not to draw attention to myself but being that I am suppose to be running a top-notch marketing firm I do need to keep up appearances. We have an underground parking garage, which houses about thirty cars. Only specific people get parking passes. Dad still runs a tight ship and likes to maintain control over most things. I have another car parked in the back corner, covered, I have a McLaren.

After a mission in Dubi I drove one and fell in love. Now I take it out on the 280 from time to time. I can get to San Jose and back quickly. It is so much fun.

Today is ordinary. I get upstairs and check my messages. I actually have two businesses I help market. Crazy enough they pay decent. Nothing like I am used to getting paid, but that work doesn't come cheap. I do my thirty minuets of work and hit the gym. Shower and get a bite to eat. Dad sends over an assignment. He likes to send me to far out in butt fuck Egypt places these days. Khovsgol Lake on the border of Mongolia and Siberia was a real treat. It was lush and green; the ride out was pleasant enough. The best part of my work is the travel. I have been all over the world. I have seen beautiful castles and seen the private collections of some of the most famous works of art. I take in everything around me, not missing one beat. I have eaten at El Celler de Can Roca in Spain, Noma in Denmark, Mirazur in France, Mamas Fish House on Maui, Tock's in Shanghai and even Los Jorritos in Arizona. I try to make the best of my trips being that some may think my line of work isn't too uplifting. He sent me out for a big meeting of buyers obtaining a large shipment of young boys. There I discovered there is a major player based out of Turkey. These rats always travel in herds. I was able to take them all out. Some of them put up a good fight. I notice no matter what language, some call me Ghost. Really builds but the self-confidence. As for the young boys, I hope they are okay.

I have always been able to turn my emotions off when it comes to work. Take nothing personal. I do pray for everyone involved. I hope that is enough to save my soul in the end.

Apparently dad was able to find an exact location of Mr. Big Shot Turkey. This time I will have to fly out, scout and wait. Waiting is the hardest sometimes, always what to do to pass the time. These assignments are not always cut and dry. Hand to hand is fun but I do enjoy a snipers perch every now and then. I have a feeling that is what is going to happen. When encountering these people in hand to hand I have a slight advantage. No one ever sees me coming. I am quick to strike and most of the time they do not have a clue what just happened. All off a sudden they just go into a coughing spell and die, or their hearts just stop. I have only had to slit a couple throats. It is not the cleanest but it leaves a message. Though they all suffer to a certain extent, no one realizes why. Its like it was just meant to happen, not that they were targeted. But this method does make it easy to move in and out of places and no one ever starts asking questions.

With flights bought, travel secure I realize I will be getting out of town just in time for Pumpkin Festival. Half Moon Bay always welcomes a million people the second weekend of October. Pumpkin Festival is a weekend filled with all things pumpkin. Pumpkin Pancakes, pumpkin bread, pumpkin ice cream, pumpkin beer and more. There are live bands, pumpkin carvings; Safeway does a weigh off for the farmer who grows the biggest pumpkin. It is a bucket list staple I think everyone should experience. As for the residents of Half Moon Bay, we usually try and get the hell out of town for it if there is not something we are obligated to be apart of.

I am Her

Growing up in Half Moon Bay this weekend was the JAM! We would rollerblade all over, cruse in the parade, dress up and socialize with everyone. The Stolo's would always through a killer party and everyone would end up at the beach for a bonfire. The town's folk would come together and endure the entire tourist for two days. The High school football team sells pancakes every morning, the softball team sells pies and most locals have a booth. I will miss the I.D.E.S. steak sandwiches though. I do love this festival, I am just not feeling it this year.

Thankfully it is only Thursday and the drive home isn't bad. I cut through Pacifica. The new tunnel is a God sent. Devils slide was getting shady, we think a kid we graduated with drove over the cliff; and with 92 being the only decent way in and out of town was getting old. Being stuck on the coast is nice but if you ever have to get out of town you do not have many options.

Danielle was already at the bar when I got in. Judy the forty-year-old hostess greeted me politely but proceeded to go on and on as if she doesn't see me once a week when I am in town. This is Danielle's and my 'go to' place to eat. Glad I am able to go unnoticed. Danielle of course has the attention of everyone around her when I approach. She moves some prep dork aside to make room for me then shoos the others away. Vincent gets us our bread with oil and vinegar per usual. I think he knows who I am. We did go to school with his kids. Regardless, I think he at least knows I am Danielle's friend.

Danielle just stares at me with a smile and I see it. Matt finally asked her the big question. They have been living together in an old fixer upper behind Main Street.

Guess they went for a sunset walk on the bluffs and he dropped down on a knee and asked. Matt is a good guy too. He was the jerk growing up but Danielle whipped him into shape. He sells stock so I know coming home to her every night is exciting for him. I am happy for them both. Danielle deserves the best. She truly cares for others. Though she enjoys typing in numbers all day long, it could be worse. She is a total tech nerd now. She really did a total flip and went from flaky space cadet to a numbers cruncher. I am honored when she asks me to be her Maid of Honor. Besides my sisters weddings none of my friends have gotten married yet. Sadly Danielle is my only real friend but still, she is the first.

She starts to dive into ideas, colors, places, and dresses. I tune out for a moment as I see a man follow a younger woman into the restaurant. Age gaps in relationships are not an issue; the red flag most people miss are the older men with young teenage girls. People just assume it is a dad or uncle. They are seated together but she never looks up. Another man joins them. An exchange is made and the original man leaves. I can't even have a nice dinner with a friend without seeing the worst in people. This is my queue to use the restroom. In the time it takes one to pee I complete my task. The girl should be safe tonight. Hopefully she has someone to call. As for the man she was currently with, he will meet his maker tonight. I get back to Danielle.

Danielle is pissed I am leaving for work. Like I had a clue what she expected me to do this weekend. I told her I would do my Maid of Honor homework during my travels. Which means when I get back I am going to have to do a crash course in whatever the hell a Maid of Honor is suppose to do. This is serious. Danielle is no joke, her expectations are high and I must deliver. This is one assignment I am actually nervous about. Like always she has already put together a binder of likes and ideas.

We eat and have a couple glasses of wine. She leaves me with her laundry list of things I need to do. I know her well enough to do exactly what she wants. And if I draw a blank I will just hack her computer and see what she already put together. I know she has at least three Pintrest boards. No one I know has privacy. No one I meet will either. It's a curse but I always have to take a look and get all the information possible.

I get three texts from Danielle the next morning. God this is going to be a job. One I will be able to commit to once I get back from my trip. I am expecting to be gone about a week. We will see. You never know sometimes. But I do know for sure that Danielle will text me every day until I get back.

I board my first flight as myself. Then as I make my way across the world Georgia comes out, Francis, Debbie, Jordan, Tasha. A well planned out task always makes for a great adventure.

Memory

My favorite name to use these days is Bella. Especially in Europe, it is so common and slang for every female. I feel like it helps me move through with ease. The first time I used Bella I was on an assignment in Bitonto, the Metropolitan City of Bari in Italy. The City of Olives is near the top of the heel of the boot. The city is cute and has some tourist attractions like the Romanesque Bitonto Cathedral, The church of San Francesco, San Gaetano, The Sylos-Labini Palace and some good places to eat. Their olive oil, wine, beer and almonds are excellent too. I was there for the Beat Onto Jazz Festival. It is a truly good time if you want to check it out. I am partial to the NOLA Jazz Festival in the states but some may argue with me.

Posing as a young Festival goer was easy. I usually get in an out of places quiet quickly but I was able to hang around and enjoy the food and music for this one. I think that it actually helped with my cover. My targets where to show up at different times and watch different bands so it was a good venue for me to kill them. I was able to eat and relax until my assignments showed up. I may have been too relaxed for this assignment but I was young and slightly cocky at this point. I feel I have maintained a humble state of mind through the years but I was just hot off a couple intense kills and was living it up on my European summer vacation.

This time I felt cute and was trying out a new topical, when applied to the skin it is immediately absorbed but take around two hours to take full affect. The topical would be applied and I would have to follow up with the results later that evening or hear about them on the news. Typically I like to see first hand the results of my work, not in the serial killer way for satisfaction, but in the clarification the job is complete sense.

During set change I was able to bump into my first target and apply the topical easily. He was so distracted by a beautiful young girl he had no idea that I basically rubbed his entire left bicep with it. I think he was relaxed in the festival environment and let his guard down but who am I to judge. When people are high on a form of drugs it does help me navigate undetected, to them I am truly not even there.

He went to talk to the young woman and thankfully she blew him off and he returned to his seat to watch the next act and so did I. About an hour later I got up to walk around and find number two.

Sadly I found number two, arm in arm with his wife accompanied by two of his bodyguards. Getting to him was a challenge. I needed to get past the bodyguards and some how touch him while his wife was there and in a spot she would not touch for at least five minuets after application.

One of the bodyguards seemed to be distracted by some of the women dancing so I made my move to go dance with these ladies. They were a group of nice girls from Germany just dancing and having a good time. They welcomed me and we danced. I started having a good time and almost forgot I somehow needed to get to the bodyguard then to my target. I was able to lead the girls to the beer line as we danced. I pretended to be Italian and acted like I didn't know much German. I wanted to look authentic as possible. We were in the beer line next to the bodyguard who was waiting on my target to purchase a drink for him and his wife. One of the girls started to yell about something exciting and bumped two of us other girls into the bodyguard who caught the pretty German girl next to me, allowing me to crash into my target. It was magically perfect. I was able to apply the topical to his lower back under his shirt; none of the wiser.

I enjoyed the next hour with my new German girl friends then went to the bathroom and never returned. The following morning I was able to check up on both my targets. The hospital was light staffed early in the morning at shift change that I was able to move in and out to confirmed both of their passing within minuets of each other. The EMT's were ruling one as a heart attack and the other as an allergic reaction. None seemed to be suspicious and it allowed me time to enjoy the end of summer in Italy.

The Lifestyle

My current assignment allowed me to try out one of my new workout challenges. I have been doing intense HITT workouts, martial arts and a lot of cardio since High School. Over the years I have changed it up with Yoga, Pilates and other weight lifting programs to help with strength and keep my body ready for anything. Knowing that I would be spending a lot of time waiting and unable to move through the city I found some workouts online. I started my days with my "Hotel Room Workout" and ended the day with something similar. I had posed motion sensors through various spots in the town to allow me some sleep. Don't let the movies fool you. Spies, assassins and other agents have to sleep. We are all human to my knowledge. Some have taken drugs to keep them up or have used other devices to keep them alert. To me there is nothing like sleep. If one is truly prepared you can take a little nap here and there. Even Telsa only spelt for a couple hours here and there and he was a genius.

With Danielle's wedding in mind I was determined to get in peek physical condition for her big day. I saw some of the dresses she wanted us to wear and I know I would have to be in shape for them to look decent. For twenty minuets every morning and occasionally throughout the day I do fifty jumping jacks, twenty-five squats, ten push-ups, ten lunges each leg, ten burpees, fifteen leg lifts and a minuet plank.

I would like to have a little more definition in my abs. I do extra abdominal sets because I really have nothing else to do.

Over the last couple years I have trained my body to accept terrible tasting food as well. I do love real Italian Gelato and the brick oven pizza from the place with the bearded lady across from the Piazza Gerolomini but on these long assignments in the middle of no where land, not able to leave my perch I have to make due with non perishables and weird paste packets full of nutrients. It is like taking vitamins, just swallow fast and not think about it. Today I am craving a pizza with pesto, goat cheese, artichoke hearts, black olives, and peppers. I am good about portion control, counting my macros and making sure I fuel my body with what it needs. I have to in this industry. There have been times I have been stuck and unable to eat properly which changes the game if you are not physically and mentally prepared.

Radio

I have been posted in the same spot for three days now. To kill time I got on the band radio and discovered there is a marine post not far from me. I have been listening in on them to pass the time between my workout sets. I did not bring a book to read, though I would have been able to read it about three times at this point. American military bases are fun to listen in on. Whenever I know there is one close by I make sure I tap in and listen, like checking in and making sure they are ok and listen to their absurd stories. Movies about these guys do not do them justice. I am so bored I find their banter entertaining though I hope no one else hacked U.S. systems. I would hope the enemy does not have my advance technology.

The group consists of about twenty-five men that have been sent to this desert waist land to gain intelligence. This is actually not your typical desert. There is a nice breeze and a body of water near by and near the river there is some vegetation. The militia heavily regulates the nicest parts; otherwise it would be a tourist attraction for sure. Marines have always fascinated me. I know a couple

Marine from Elementary school. Growing up we stayed in contact via Facebook. They are good times. This group makes me laugh. Besides the macho bullshit of who is bigger they all get along well. I really do not know how to describe their dynamic but I will say I love listening to their odd life stories and games they play. They are truly a family unit, are in sync with one another and have this wonderful bond.

Some of the guys in this group are Ivy League College Grads and a couple joined right-out of High School. They all have nicknames for each other; which I love. I really have no idea what anyone's real name is and want to know how a couple came to inherit their nicknames. They remind me of my family, but much closer to one another than I am with my sisters. I wonder what nickname they would make up for me. Hopefully not something fearful like most of the names I have been called. Though I am the last person most people see before they die. The most unsettling thing I have ever been called is Arae. It is a female demon of curses, particularly of the curses placed by the guilty, called up from the underworld to take them away. It scared me because it could be true. The definition fits, the dammed killing the dammed. I guess it just rubbed me the wrong way that night. I haven't killed up close and personal since that.

Late in the afternoon five of the men make their way through the one of the streets where I am located. And by street I mean dirt road with make shift buildings on each side. There are only a handful of buildings of what was once a beautiful city. It has been abandoned for a couple years now since this group of thugs started to use the space to store drugs and people for their new gang business. The Marines start clearing each building and report back their findings. Marines and Seals are very systematic in their methods. Though they are ruff and wild out here in the middle of nowhere they are precise and skilled. They are professionals and do not want to die. Though I have seen some Marines begging for death due to extreme circumstances, these men are precise and organized. Once they make their way to me I get a closer look at them through my scope. I know they could never find me so I take advantage and check them out. They could be right on top of me and have no clue. I'm good at hiding. I wish I knew what they were searching for; I may be able to lead them directly to it. As they make their way to the third building I pick up a heat signature down the street. The enemy is coming fast and furious. They set off a couple of my motion sensors.

Within seconds the Marines recognize the situation and dive into one of the buildings to take cover. They hide in the third building. It has three stories. Windows have been boarded up but small holes that allow minimal light, dirt floors. Sadly there is no way for them to assess their situation from their location but I stay alert and watch. There is a back door they do not know about. I have the layout memorized. If they stay calm and wait it out they may be fine. One man stays hidden behind the door as he tries to peek out and see who and what is going on.

As I watch the enemy start to slow I hear a change in dynamic within the marine team. Before it was all bros and equals. Now it is Master and Sargent's. The one they call "Doc" is barking orders. Stay low and wait. "Boomer" is calling out ideas of strike options. All five heart rates start to climb. They need to just chill out and stay put. "Dad" starts to suggest retreat options and "Kid" Starts to pray. Why is no one calling for back up?

I hope the bad guys don't come down this far. I think the gunfire was for show. These vigilantes act like it is the Wild West sometimes and I know they are hear to round up the last of the drugs in the old bakery a couple buildings down. I do not think my Marines were spotted. But I do not want to take any chances. These guys are some of the best but even they wouldn't survive the army that is headed their way. These guys look like they are ready to blow everything up after they get what they need. This is the biggest group I have seen come through here the last couple days. The marines start accessing their options but I do not like any of them, none of them are good. They are great at what they do but do not have the information they need to get out of this situation. I know now their Intel was wrong. They should have never been searching these buildings. What where they even looking for anyway? I know for a fact there is nothing here but the drugs and why would Marines care about foreign drug? I have been through this deserted town with a fine tooth-comb and there really is not anything here for them. Damn, I should have been paying more attention to their conversations. This abandoned town does not posses anything the United States Government would be interested in. Even what I am looking for is not here; yet. I just know we had different missions. If only my person of interest would show his face so I could kill two birds with one stone and get out of here with these guys. My gut is telling me this was a set up. As "Kid" starts on his second Hail Mary I call over their coms. I think the food deprivation is making me cranky.

Boomer: "What the fuck. Who the hell are you?"

Me: "Don't get your silkies in a bunch. Just shut up and Listen"

Doc: "What, how......."

Me: "There is a group of three jeeps slowing down but headed straight for you. I think you may have been spotted. There are eleven total, all heavily armed and there are weapons attached to each Jeep. Jeeps each have a driver and a gun man so that leaves you with five men possible on foot in about five minuets."

"They have come to a stop"

Though I cannot see what they are doing I can tell by they're hand movements on their heat signatures they are trying to figure out who and what the hell just happened... and where I came from. They seem to be using some sort of sign language to communicate with each other. I am unable to focus on what they are saying to one another because I am staying alert to what are drug dealers are doing.

There is no time for explanations but I need to figure out a way for them to listen to me. I realize now I have never been good with people but I cannot let anything happen to these men. For what it is worth they have been my saving grace the last couple days. I feel like I am their creepy stalker but mother figure having to protect them. I rack my brain to my rescue and negotiations training. Shit that was a waste.

So I just start talking…more like rambling.

Me: "I have been listening in on you guys for the last couple of days. Sorry but I am not going to let you just die. I know every inch of this square mile and I am going to tell you how to get out of here. Has anyone called in for help yet?"

Turbo: "Why should we trust you?"

Me: "We are on the same side more or less. Listening to you guys over the last couple days has made my mission bearable. I am usually alone, all the time. You guys are better than Family Guy. Besides the radio station that only gets one rock station, I have been listening to your banter for entertainment."

Now I am like a sad little sister being ignore by her brothers.

Turbo: "Then you know our Intel was bad?"

Me: " I just realized that when I saw the men driving up. I will investigate the error once my mission is over. If you can believe it I know how to get you out but you are all going to have to start taking some deep breaths. Your heart rates are spiking and I need you calm and level headed to make it out. Hold ON….."

"I am back, the base is sending a HUM V or Jeep transport with two men to come get you. I radioed your location of pick up."

Doc: "Why are you helping us? What is your mission solider?"

Me (silly but dramatic): "My mission is to rid the world of evil."

"I am helping you because I believe you are here on false pretenses and I want to make sure you boys get home safe. There is no need for you to die today and or get in the way of my assignment."

Turbo: "Thanks, who are you?"

Me: "I am just a Ghost. A loan wolf if you will."

Boomer chimes in: "Don't go stealing my goals lady."

Boomer is the man whore of the group. He loves the challenge of getting a woman naked. His stories haven't been too fun to listen too. The only thing is he is honest in his conquests. He is not like the one guy from back in High School. Still, I do not have to ever hear him recite all of his pick up lines ever again. That is something to look forward too.

Kid: "Please make sure my family is okay."

Kid is the sensitive guy of the group. His whole life has been to take care of others. Even now when he is in a tight situation he is worried about his family. The couple stories he told about his wife and kids were so romantic. They are high school sweethearts. He went straight into the Marines to make money for his family. He thought about maybe trying something else but know this was the path he was meant to be on. It is what it is for him. Simple. He has a little girl and another one on the way. I am going to make sure he gets home. I know what having your dad apart of your life means to a girl, even if he teaches her to be a killer.

Me: "You are all getting out of this. Trust me I have been stuck in worse. Kid, you will go home to your wife and kids. Your wife will always be waiting at the front door waiting to make sure your okay. Your kids will have an amazing father. Sadly your girls are never going to date or have a life with their four Uncles guarding them."

Dad tisks at me over the COM.

Me: "Dad you are going to end up marring some gypsy woman that puts her shit all over. It's going to drive you crazy but your going to love her too much to care. SO don't Tsk me again to I will be sure to be the one to make the introduction. Boomer you're going to sleep with another hundred women I am sure of it. So just please calm down."

Turbo: "You are so sure, how can you be so sure?"

Me: "I have seen the bad, the Dante's Inferno type stuff since I was in high school. Where I come from and what I do, it is always bad. You guys are good at what you do. And if you listen to me you will be out of here in fifteen min. They are slowing down."

Turbo: " With all the darkness you see how do you go on? How do you find the light?"

I have to really think about this for a second. Am I totally emotionless? What have I become? Can I even see the good anymore? I am happy for Danielle and Matt but do I see light in the end or darkness? Do I live in her happiness or do I have my own? Can I have my own? I kill with no regard. Like it really isn't that big of a deal. I know Turbo is fighting some inner demons. Did I just put myself at risk for them because like the books I read I imagine myself being apart of the story? Now in this real life story I am making it my own? I overheard Turbo and Boomers conversations the other night. A couple years back they took out what seemed like a small village of really bad men. It has always stuck with them. They can only talk to each other about it. It was their first kills and it was gruesome. Boomer sleeps his way through the pain.

Women seem to calm him as he puts it. I am interested in seeing what these guys really look like. Putting a face to the voice. I have a feeling Boomer is easy on the eyes. Turbo goes to confession and tries to deal with what he saw. I don't think either one is doing a good job. Sadly my first kill was satisfying. May be I am void of emotion. Then it hits me.

Me: " Listen Turbo, I am going to ask you one thing and you all must promise me this and I will get you out of here. Promise."

All but not in unison: "Promise"

Me: "I know you are all Island boys, stationed on Oahu but when all is said and done; when you get back you need to fly over to Maui for me. Rent a car and take it to the Shave Ice Stand in Kihei. It is called Ululani's Hawaiian Shaved Ice and it is by the ABC Store. It's on South Kihei. Make your way around sunset. Sit on the benches close to the corner and watch the sun go down. The ocean is beautiful at this time. If you want you can even walk across the street to the beach and chill. There is where I find peace with all I have seen and done. There I still see beauty in the world. There I know everything is going to be okay, even if it is just for those few minuets at sunset. Also, there is no denying the sugar rush I get from the guava and vanilla ice cream, that life is great if food can be that good."

Dad: "What the Fuck? Shaved Ice?"

Me: "Sorry you seem like a root beer float kind of guy."

Doc:" It's a deal, now get us out of here."

The Great Escape

We hear gunfire and I get into position. I am ready to return fire if needed. Safely tucked away in my invisible clock (sorry I like Harry Potter) no one will know where the shots where fired from. The criminals just shoot at stuff then things can get out of hand fast and if there are others in the area the death toll rises. Careless criminals make for great news stories.

Me: " You are going to stay low. In two breaths you're going to make your way through the side hallway to the left. Doc, that is your left as you are facing the south wall. Walk cautiously now."

"You are going to head until you see the old blue door. Open the door and stay to the right of it. The passage will lead you to what seems like a kitchen with a bed in it"

Doc: "We are here"

Me: " Now go to the wall with all the rusted pots on them. Slide the cabinet they are on over."

The boys make noise but I do not think anyone can hear. The enemy seems to be walking the street, kicking over garbage and taking a smoke break. I think they think the town is empty so they are just acting like adolescents.

Me: "Now make your way to the very end. You will come out onto a street. Once outside stay to the west of the street in the shadows and run north. Run Like hell."

As the door opens I see two men approaching from the south end of the road rounding the corner from an abandoned alley. Shit. They snuck up on me. While I am watching the others take a bloody smoke break these guys must have gone on a little adventure and cut through the ally way. As Turbo brings up the rear and exits the door I speak again.

Me: "Turbo, when I count to three stop in your tracks and take a deep breath."

What seems like the slowest, drawn out way I count:" One, Two, Three." Turbo does exactly what I asked and as I exhale the number three I send two bullets past his left ear just above his shoulder nailing both of the men heading toward him. Turbo exhales, turns then runs like hell. We all know the sound of my shots has alerted the other men to a possible threat. Thankfully the rescue Hum V is approaching and about to pick up my men. I do not think I will have to fire any more shots but I am ready just in case.

The boys are picked up as the wind picks up. The dust from the street masks my boy's swift get-away. The enemy finds their two men dead. Bullets through and through and they have no idea where it came from. One of the guys is trying to search for heat signatures. No luck. Smoke break is over and they load up, leaving the dead men to rot, with half of the drugs secured they take off in the direction they came. Sadly, none of the men traveling today, where anyone of importance to me. I hope my target shows up soon. This excitement makes me more anxious to be done with this assignment. Something about it all does not feel right. I do not know if I am just hangry for Italian pizza, getting my period, but something about being assigned here the same time a Marine group is investigating the abandoned town just sits with me wrong.

If you can believe it I do sleep on the job. I am human and need to sleep and eat. I have monitors posted to wake me if there is any movement so I do not miss my target. I wake up a couple hours later and get a snack. I can sleep anywhere and at anytime. My internal clock is a Patek Philippe. I turned off my COM once my Hula Boys where safely on their way knowing they were in safe hands. Now that I am rested and my tummy is full I think I will check in on them. I am interested to see their perspective on what happened and investigate why they were even sent to my little town, at the same time as me.

The rescue team has a million questions. Once they made it safe back at base they were bombarded with questions. One being "Who in the hells mom called requesting you boys to be picked up? This is a Marine mission not the middle school bus station." At first all of them started in on their version of what happened. All five were going a mile a minute. Then Richard got pissed and made them each tell their story one by one. Doc was the first to go. He was precise and accurate. Boomer used a lot of curse words and Turbo was in the clouds. I don't think any of them realized what happened but he was defiantly still lost about it. No one could figure out who I was or what I was doing out there and why I saved them. Richard concluded I had to be an American spy to save them. Though I am American I do not serve just the American people. I do not think the organization I work for is even American. I think they are based out of Prague but that is my own conspiracy theory. I serve all people, the Good people. The other Marines seemed to join in and had many theories but then in the chaos the Kid spoke and shut everyone up.

Kid dead serious and flat toned: "She was our Guardian Angel. She saved us. Nothing else matters."

Silence hit the twenty-five Marines like a tone of bricks. I was taken aback. No one has ever referred to me as anything like that before. Hell a man has never even called me pretty. But to be called an Angel was beyond anything I could have ever imagined. I felt it in my heart. At that point I knew I loved these men. I promised myself I would look out for them. They were my Hula Boys. I knew we had a bond from then on. Even though they may never know me. They knew me. It could have been my tummy craving peperoni and gelato, the emotions of being a female but this experience gave me hope and made my heart feel warm for the first time.

After a couple more hours of getting cleaned up and coming off the high the guys passed out. I took that time to do some research of my own. I wanted to know where they got their Intel from and why these five specifically where sent on this mission. I know they have all been on the same team in the past but they have never been a five-man team with such a specific mission, to gain information on the layout of the town did not seem like the standard Marine assignment.

First of all a satellite image would have given them fifty percent of the information they needed. This town has been abandoned for years. A lot of these places come and go. There is a herd that comes through. No government really owns anything and unless people make it a home and build a community, trade doesn't happen and it never develops into anything more. Not like Arizona, once AC became a regular in home feature the State boomed. Everyone wanted to move there. Highways where paved and malls built. Not so much happening here. Here would be a great location of a horror film.

In my search I came across the boys files. I debated myself if what was inside was important. But for the sake of making sure I left no stone unturned; I read each file.

Doc is Robert. He is in his forties. He entered into the Marines out of college. He has Bachelors in Psychology from the University of Oklahoma where he was born and raised. Native American by blood, he currently has a wife, retired schoolteacher and two kids in college. He is very active in his tribal community still and likes to stay true to some of his traditional ways his Grandmother taught him in regards to food and respecting the Earth. His oldest child goes to Michigan State and his youngest goes to Oklahoma. He is the Master Sergeant. I think I have heard him called Major before. His file states he is an explosive expert, skilled in bomb making and defusing. He is the older and wiser one of the crew. He calls the shots and his record is spotless. Model Marine living the dream. Close to full retirement. Looks like he has had many opportunities to take a safe desk assignment but has turned them all down. He sounds like the man of the people. A true Chief and Leader. His tribe would be proud and his new Marine Tribe looks up to him.

Boomer, our Hawaiian Playboy is in fact Polynesian. College Football player, University of Hawaii, Majored in Communications. He is your stereotypical Hawaiian surfer, all American boy. Ohana is important to him. He still lives with his parents in Pearl City rather than living on base. He does have a distinct scar across is back from a bar fight when he first enlisted. There is a mark on his record but I am not going to take the time to dive into the why of that. He likes explosives and is skilled in the art of all things that go BOOM. Thus the nickname, though Nate is a good name too. Nate's always tend to be attractive. He has a tendency to blow things up and ask questions later.

James is the Dad of the group. OCD does not even begin to describe his personality. His tests and psych evaluations are off the charts. He is precise and analytical, everything with reason. He is a minimalist by far. No wonder the guys call him "buzz kill" I do not think he gets humor with all the notes documented in his file. He is an amazing marksman, tested top of his class. Graduated MIT early, yet there is no answer given to why he joined the marines with his track record. It is as if he woke up one day and said "I'm going to be a Marine." Then did it. I am sure Doc has made some conclusions. His status states he is currently the Gunny Sargent. Which fits his personality. He must make quick accurate decision, enforce discipline and plan daily activities. He was made for it. His awkward personality does not seem to affect the rest of the group. No one seems to care he is odd and has issues communicating in simple language. The other men seem to look to him for the exact answer though they need a little help navigating his sentence structure.

Logan the Kid is one of my favorites. His wife is a nurse; they both want to help people. He comes from a mixed home and currently has a mixed family. Though what he has faced in his past he does not let it get in the way of what he wants. Growing up African American and now having a Hispanic wife seems like it would be tough but he lets nothing stop him from his goals. His parents where hard working blue collared people that defiantly raised him right. Hawaii is a good place for his family. The culture is welcoming and family based. He joined the marines out of High School because he couldn't afford college. It worked out for him because he got his degree in arms and met his wife. I guess she was the one giving vaccinations before one of his deployments. Totally Pearl Harbor movie "AWE." They are both young. As corporal he is looking to advance fast. From his file it looks like he is on the fast track. Good marks in everything. He has a daughter with another one on the way.

I know I am side tracking myself from the task at had but learning about these men interests me. I really need to start bringing books with me to pass the time. Now that they think so highly of me I need to learn more about them, only to better protect them. I have no movement in town so what else am I going to do? I can repeat my workout as soon as I am done here. These files do not revile any thing I have not already learned. I find pleasure in researching the tiniest of details.

Turbo is Mr. Eric. He is my age. He is the total Red White and Blue type personality, sense of duty, brave. Was an orphan as a kid and was placed in different Catholic centers to help him get an education before a Marine family adopted him when he was thirteen. He only lives on the bare necessities. His adopted parents didn't even want him to follow in their footsteps as Marines but them adopting him was life changing for him. His mother is a retired Sargent that wanted him to become a Doctor but there was no way he could honor her wishes. He found his calling the day they adopted him and have been there for him ever since. He hasn't spoken to them yet about what happened on his first mission. I think his parents both know when it is time he will come around. Their files are both thick. I do not have time to dive into that. Eric is an excellent marks man. Sniper training. Special ops tabs are listed in his file. They may take some hacking to get into later.

For the most part they are all top of their class, excellent Marines. I haven't been able to find any info on to why they were thrown together and or why they were sent to my town. It is day four and my mark has not shown up yet. I am hoping it is not like freshman year at Santa Clara State. I waited two weeks in the spring for a three-man hit. I missed one week of school after spring break and had so much homework to make up. Life was simpler then. Instead of writing a paper on the Importance of Andy Warhol to the Pop Art Movement I am hacking into a government server to stalk five men I just saved. Good times.

I cannot look at the computer anymore so I decide to COMM in and see how the boys are doing today. Everything seems to have gone back to normal. Richard, the head of the operation is pissed off. He believes they were sent out to die or to be set up. He has a flare for the dramatic but he may be right. Nothing has come out of them being here except my five boys being possibly pinned down and lead to die, if it wasn't for me. Shit, what did I do? I am going to have to fill my dad in on all this when I get back.

Not realizing it, there is a voice coming over the COMM. I hear him say my name a couple times before I am able to respond.

Turbo: "Angel, Angel are you there?"

I do not think it is safe or wise for me to respond. I have to pretend I did not help them and let them move on. No one needs to know of my existence. It felt good while it lasted.

Turbo: " Angel, I know you can hear me. Thank you for saving us. A life is important and you saved five. Not sure where you are or why you are here but I am Thankful you got stuck listening to us. Thanks for watching our backs. We owe you one."

Me: "You owe me nothing"

Turbo: "Your really out there? You're real? Some of the guys think we imagined you. But Richard confirms you called barking orders at him to rescue us and everyone is too scared of Richard to argue. Richard calls you our mom. He claims he has never been yelled at like that before."

Me: "I'm real and I didn't yell at him. I was stern. But saving you was selfish. I do not regret it. But it could have compromised my mission. (After a long awkward pause) And for what it is worth, your first mission was a blood bath. What you saw I don't wish on anyone. Your actions were appropriate for your circumstances. In my line of work the bad comes with the good: A kill to save a life of an innocent. Try to see what you did right instead of what you saw. I really can't say you ever forget. But how your feeling means you are human. And you are a good human."

Over the next twenty-four hours I listen in to the boys. Richard searches for answers but comes up empty. He makes some intense and angry phone calls in which gets them pulled and sent home. I am going to start my search again but I like Richard doing some legwork too. There is nothing from my mark. Three men returned to retrieve the bodies earlier. As they were moving them into the jeep I detonated a landmine and took them all out. Hopefully that did not scare off my mark. They know U.S. soldiers are near buy so there is nothing to raise suspicion. They still have a load of drugs to pick up and need to come for it. They tend to rotate drugs every couple of weeks but I hope I do not get stuck here that long.

Eric/ Turbo calls over the COMM randomly through out the next day. He talks to me about what it was like growing up before he was adopted. He tells me this one story about one home he was staying at. The family was so nice but the mom did not know how to cook. She tried so hard every night to cook a good dinner. Every night at the dinner table the kids and father would smile and muscle down as much as they could. Then every morning the dad would give the kids extra food money to get a big snack on the way home from school so no one was really hungry for dinner. He laughed pretty hard telling me he loved to hit up this one local burger place. The owner would give him an extra bag of onion rings to take home because he was such a loyal customer. Then one day the mom got ill. He offered to cook dinner. From that point until he cooked dinner every night and made lunches for everyone until he was removed from the home a month later.

I feel guilty for not responding but I have to keep listening. Eric/ Turbo COMMs in later in the evening to say good night. He hopes that I have accomplished my mission and he thanks me once again. He calls me Angel. That is my nickname. I am going to go with it. If they really knew me I think it would not be so lovely of a name.

Me: "Thank you Turbo. Goodnight"

Oh why did I respond? Kicking myself in the face here! Why do I feel so guilty? My emotions are all over the place. I think I am getting stir crazy or going to get my period or in need of some real food. I am going to have to ask for quicker missions in the immediate future. Space these long ones out. This assignment is wearing on me. After this I have to jump over to Spain for an overnight then I can head home, or may be I'll go visit my dad.

Turbo: "How's your hideaway today Angel?"

Me: "Nothing has changed. Same old same old"

Turbo: "I am glad you got stuck out here with us even though your mission is dragging on. May be one day you can teach me to shoot like that one day."

Me: "From your file I think you may be just as skilled if not better than myself. You have excellent scores."

Turbo: "Oh, so you have been looking into us."

Me: "Guilty"

Turbo: "So anything juicy?"

Me: "You are all very different but boring. Per your files there is nothing I could not have already assessed from listening in on you."

Turbo: "Since you know about us, what about you?"

What is this? Is this flirting? How do I even go about this? I should not have responded. What is wrong with me? Why did he want to know about me?

Me: "I am average in every way possible"

Turbo: "I have a hard time believing that. Do you have family or are you like me"

Me: "I have family and so do you."

Turbo: "Are you my age?"

Me: "Yes"

Turbo: "What is your favorite baseball team?"

Me: "The Giants."

Turbo: "Sorry we cant be friends anymore"

Me: "What?"

Turbo: "Just kidding. You saved my life so now I have to be friends with you. Sadly I can not forgive you for being a Giants Fan, Dodgers all the way"

Me: "May be saving you wasn't well thought out."

Turbo: (after a big heavy laugh) "Seriously where did you learn to shoot like that?"

Me: "Shooting just runs in my family"

Turbo: "I can not believe you are that good and not apart of the Marines or Seals. Are you a spy?"

Me: "Why do you assume I am not apart of your organization somehow?"

Turbo: "The way you talk, your lingo. You have no formal training. At least with the US government"

Me: "I am not a spy"

Turbo: "Bummer, that would have been hot."

Me: "I am defiantly not hot. Average, remember?"

Turbo: "Anyone that can send a bullet from God knows where millimeters from a surface to a precise target is Heavenly to me. And you did it twice."

Me: "Thank you for the complement but that wasn't even the hardest shot I have ever taken... not to brag"

What am I doing? I think being here I have officially lost it. I am just having a conversation about my life that is suppose to be secret with some guy I have never met. Okay, sanity just left the building.

I have movement ahead of me. Please be who I am here for. The vehicle approaches fast. There are three men in the vehicle. They start to slow as they pass my last explosion. All three get out and start to survey the previous carnage. As I switch my COMM and listen in they are all calm going back and forth. They think it was one of their landmines left over from a couple months back. They are so careless they have no idea that they are actually correct it did belong to them; I just placed it myself. I notice as the third man that comes around the wreckage is my guy. I listen in on their conversation. Something about having to hurry back and report on where their men went. Something about making up for loss of lives with more lives. And there is mention of a shipment. I have enough Intel. I let three bullets fly. Then I detonate the new bomb I placed in the wreckage a couple hours before my nap. Things work out nicely. Or as my dad says "Perfect preparation makes for a successful mission."

I totally ditched Turbo. I switch frequencies and realize he is gone. Bummer. I start to pack up. Now I can get to Spain then home faster. I know Danielle is going to have a million things for me to do and I have to finish my checklist still.

I am mostly packed up when I decided to take a break and remove all evidence. Now I am done with this place. I have been listening in on the boys and Richard has come to a dead in on his Intel search. I guess he hit some classified only files that he does not have access too. He made some calls and is waiting. Richard really called in some favors. The guys still have not been shipped out. It is weird they have not packed up and left. They have no mission and are running out of supplies. I know they have a transport scheduled to come late tomorrow night. Richard is just frantic and not liking being in the dark. Dramatic. I will make sure I check in on them even after I leave just in case and of course bring my dad into the loop.

Turbo calls for me later that evening.

Turbo: "Goodnight Angel. Hope everything is okay and you did not just ditch me because I am not as cool as you hoped"

Me: "Goodnight. I just had to take care of something real fast that's all"

Turbo: "Are you done here?"

Me: "For now"

Turbo point blank: "How many people have you killed?"

This is not something I have ever been asked and took me by surprise. I am afraid to tell him because I have never really thought about it. I think he has an idea of what I do but I am afraid he will be disappointed in me. Or sad I am that person. I don't want to be associated with my number count but what I do to help others. In all reality he has no clue who I am and I am never going to talk to him again; so why not?

Me: "The lives I have taken have made the world a better place. If I gave you a number you would not call me Angel anymore"

Turbo: "What you did for me and they guys made you our Angel. Nothing will ever change that"

Me: "Thank you Eric"

Turbo: "Do you kill only bad guys?"

Me: "Yes"

Turbo: "I'm going to miss talking to you"

Me: "Me too"

Turbo: "Please don't forget us"

Me: "Never. But please try and stay safe for a while. I have some things I have to do so I can't be watching you all the time."

Turbo: "Do you watch us?"

Me: "No I can't see you. I just can listen in."

Turbo: "Okay. Be safe and thank you"

Me: "Aloha"

Going Aloha

S pain was nice. My assignment took no time at all. I stayed for a couple more days to enjoy the food, take in some sights and get some Maid of Honor stuff taken care of. Danielle is going love me. I picked up some great treats in Girona. Flying back to the states I make some changes and decide to go visit my dad before heading home for good. I miss him, need to fill him in on what happened but I would be lying to myself if I didn't want to go for other reasons.

Dad currently lives in Maui. Yes, in Kihei. He literally lives down the road from Ululani's. Mom and Dad bought a condo in the building we used to vacation when we were younger. They bought it and used it as a get away for their retirement. When mom died dad moved into it permanently. He has become one hundred percent immersed in the culture. It is great. He spear fishes, lives in his canoe and occasionally takes assignments. He has to keep busy.

Maui is actually not a hot spot so dad will hit Oahu now and then when big shipments come in. Other than that he is a man of the land. His business choices have left him with a comfortable life to do as he pleases. Thankful to him, I am there now. But I am going to keep on going. I have nothing else to do. Once in San Francisco I hit the office for a shower and a change of bags. I have a full closet in my spare room at the office. I also have to unload some machinery, clean it and get some food before my flight to Hawaii takes off. Instead of going home I sleep at the office and head to the airport in the morning. No need to make the drive back and forth over the hill if I don't have to.

I booked first class to Maui. I make good enough money with my Marketing Business I can indulge in the finer things; extra leg room. I also like Hawaiian Airlines first class. Boarding my flight I text dad I am coming. Just in case. I never want to walk in on something I can never un-see. He has been dating these last couple months. My little sister was out to see him this summer and she had to conference us girls in on everything that happened after her vacation. She was a little upset about it but I think it is good for dad. He needs the distraction otherwise he would just be on a non stop killing spree and that is not healthy.

The flight was easy, movie, food, some light reading. I did my research on the passengers of the flight the night before so I know who and what is aboard. I have to know everything. Dad /James would be proud. I checked in on them last night and found out they made it back to base. Their trip home was not as nice as mine. They were granted some time off after a series of questions when they returned. Richard is still on the hunt. It sounds like the guys are just tired. They plan to recoup then hit the next mission hard.

After landing I grab the jeep dad left for me at the airport and head over to his place. No word from him so who knows what's up. Driving through the sugar cane fields, which are no longer fields, makes me sad. I used to love this drive. Now it is just flat out sad. I know dad will have food at home so I don't stop at Safeway.

He's out, left a note he wont be back for a couple days. I go into the guest room and dump my things, change and check in on the guys one last time before I hit the beach. They will be landing in a couple hours. They are really coming and are keeping their promise. My heart jumps for joy. Sadly they will never know how close they are to me. Regardless. It makes me feel good.

The ocean is perfect though the afternoon wind in starting up. I make my way down the beach. After the long flight a swim was just what my body needed. I think I am going to walk down to the ABC Store for a couple things. Maybe take a peak at the guys. Just to put a face to a name.

As I make my way down I know they are going to get there and have a surprise waiting. I mailed out a note and some money to the stand. I wrote: 'Please keep this money is for five of the bravest Marines I have ever met. They will come visit and order. Please treat them on me and give them the other note inside.' As they walk up I know the girls who work there will know who I am talking about. I was able to find a picture of all five in one of Richards files and I sent it in with my note. After they order the girls will give them my note. I am so excited. I hope I am not being creepy.

I get to the building next to all the canoes and I see them. They are all sitting at the purple bench closest to the beach. They are looking down. One of them is reading my note. I take a deep breath. Holy cow they are really here. I decide to head over and get a shaved ice. My favorite, Guava with vanilla ice-cream. After I order the girls in the back are all giggling and talking about the five marines. They are going on and on about the mysterious letter and how they really came. They put the guys picture I sent up in the window. I just stare at it. The girls are in awe and excited the "hot" Marines showed up on their shift.

I take my shaved ice and sit a couple tables away. They guys are silent. They are all lost in thought. I sit and eat my ice as if I am minding my own business. Boomer gets up to get some more napkins. He sees me and smiles. I smile back.

Boomer: "Would you care to sit with us?"

Me totally surprised and looking around knowing there is no one else near me: "Excuse me?"

Boomer: "Would you like to come sit with us? I wouldn't be a gentleman if I left a lady siting alone"

Me totally suprised: " umm sure"

What am I doing? I take a deep breath and get up and go sit with them. I end up siting next to Boomer with my back facing the street. Not the most comfortable seat for me logistic wise but since I am in the company of five marines I think I am safe. I am siting closest to the beach with Turbo across from me, next to him is Doc, the Kid and Dad moves to the other side of Boomer. I look up at all of them and smile. I am so out of my element. Eric smiles and we make our introductions.

Dad dives right into why they are all here. They tell me about the note. When they ordered the girl behind the counter told them that Angel left a note for them. Eric never takes his eyes off me.

Turbo: "I saw you walk up from the beach. Do you live around here?"

Me: "No my dad does. I am just visiting."

Turbo: "You like this place?"

Me: "It is my favorite. I make it a habit to come here when I arrive and as much as possible when I am in town"

Turbo: "What flavor did you get?"

Me: "Guava"

Turbo: "With vanilla ice-cream"

All eyes are on me at once. I know why. I feel the weight of them. They are all dealing with what happened and being here now, with a girl that ordered guava I hope I did not give myself away. But then there is a calm that falls over everyone. Eric hands me my note. I take the time to read it even though I know exactly what it says.

> *Boys,*
>
> *I am glad you made the trip. I was worried you might have forgotten me. While you sit here look around, smell the ocean air. This is the light I dream about when there is darkness around me. I miss you all. Please try and stay safe.*
>
> *Always your Angel*

I look up and all eyes are on me again. For being invisible my whole life this feels so weird. I cannot wrap my head around what is going on. My cheeks are hot and my stomach is in knots. I just wanted to come and check in on them. Never did I think I would be invited to their table. My skin feels hot and not just from the sun.

Me barley to push the words out: "She saved you" is all I could manage to say.

Doc: "She had been listening in on us. I think she has a place in her heart for us now."

Me: "I believe that."

Kid: "She was looking out for us. I pray someone is always looking out for her."

Boomer: "We all got this to honor her."

Boomer lifted up his shirtsleeve to reveal a tattoo. Tears start to fill my eyes. They did that for me. All of them did. They all have the same one. It is a simple set of angel wings in black. Doc has his on his bicep, Dad on his forearm, the Kid on his ribs and Turbo over his heart. The tears trickle out after I see Turbo's location. I know we made a connection. It means the world to me to know these men love me so. I do not regret coming here today. They notice my emotional lapse and pay no mind. I think they feel it too. Boomer seems relieved to express his gratitude to Angel to someone other than his brothers.

I let a moment pass before I ask what flavors the boys picked. They seem thankful I asked. It lightens the mood. Turbo ordered strawberry with vanilla ice cream, such a safe choice. Doc and Dad got the root beer floats, which made me giggle. They all looked at me sideways, I feel like I am blowing my cover at this point. Boomer got Guava, Lychee and Coconut with vanilla ice cream and the Kid got Orange Cream with vanilla ice cream. Each choice nails their personalities. This makes me smile.

The Kid goes on to tell me this place is exactly how I described it. He thinks it is a great spot to just be present. The wind from earlier has died down and the sun has started to set. They all get up to throw their trash away and tell me it is time. A little confused they all look at the beach.

Dad: "She thought it would be nice for us to watch the sunset from the beach. Would you care to join us?"

Me: "If all of you are okay with it I would love to."

Turbo leans in closer to me: "Thank you for coming. I feel as if she sent you to us."

Oh sweet heart if you only knew. I walk across the street with them. All such gentlemen, it is very overwhelming for me to have this much attention, especially male attention. For work I have always been in disguise but now I am me, plain old me. I have no idea what to do. At the beach we all stand and watch the sun go down. I take a step back to look at the boys. Each one is exactly how I imagined them. I love them all. I care for them as if they are my brothers. We share something that no one can take away from us.

Noticing Doc I can see the lines on his face have grown from when the picture was taken. He is tired. He is a strong man but even looking him in the eye earlier I can see he has seen much. He hides it well. I bet he was a looker ten years ago. He inhales the sunlight like it is air he will never have again. All the guys are in this daze.

They are really here to heal. The promise to me is how I know they are going to be okay.

Boomer is every bit as handsome as I thought. His picture doesn't do him justice. He is muscular and has the perfect caramel brown skin. His dark features are accented with his dark hair. It looks like he needs a cut, but the messiness works for him. He has a deep voice that I know works wonders with the ladies.

Kid is a cross between Shemar Moore and Kevin Hart. He is easy on the eyes but has this goofy smile that just makes you want to smile too. Along with the angel wings he has a tattoo of his wife's name and his daughters foot prints. I imagine where the second set of prints will go. Kid gives off such a calm vibe it is relaxing being around him. I can tell he is an asset to the team with just his pretense.

Dad is wound up so tight I bet he shits diamonds. He is always looking around accessing every avenue. I would take him for my recon if he would only relax. I notice that at this moment he is as calm as he can get. Not fully relaxed but breathing slowly. He is looking out at the waves and I think he is healing. He is letting go. His shoulders start to inch down. I think among his brothers he can let loose and that is the reason he joined the marines, to be around people that can calm him. He needs these guys. His mind is on overdrive but they allow him to focus on other things. They allow him to escape himself.

Turbo caught me off guard. His name fits him to a T. He looks like Prince Eric from the little mermaid. As he looks over the water I imagine he is looking for her.

Looking for me. If he only knew plane Jane here was his Angel. He is tall dark and handsome. He is by no means exotic. Something about him just makes me happy. I think the last couple days when we would talk. It was like I finally met someone who could know who I was and what I did. He did not judge me but liked me for me. Hell I saved his life so he may even love me. Not the love like Eric and Ariel but still it is something.

The sun goes down slow. It is as if God is allowing them the longest moments possible to enjoy this moment. I just want to give them all a hug. I have never been the affectionate type but I love these guys. After the sun sets we all just stand there until we cant really see anymore.

Doc turns to me and orders, "Where can we get a beer?"

My laugh made them all laugh and with that I joined them in their soccer mom van and we headed south. I took them to Shaka Pizza. I think I was just hungry but it was a good call on my part. I am still in shock how the night went. We ordered so much food and beers just kept coming. We made buddies with some of the locals. Some which know my father and gave all the guys a hard time. One old man told Boomer the last sight he may ever see is my dad drowning him in the cove. It was a sure laugh.

The boys were upset with me that I had failed to mention earlier that my father is a retired Marine. They had a million questions for me. Especially Turbo. We actually had something in common other than killing people. I told them about learning to shoot with my sisters and dad. How he made us all learn how to change a tire before we were allowed to take the care out for the first time alone. They loved the story I told about our camping trip in La Honda one summer. My sisters are fairly easy to deal with. My older one is go with the flow though my youngest is a handful. Us girls had a tent and my parents had a tent right next to us. Come midnight we are all woken up. Someone is in our campsite making all sorts of noise. I figure it is raccoons. I know dad will take care of it but my sisters do not let me fall back asleep. Then all of a sudden we heard shouting. Apparently Half Moon Bay High Schools Varsity Football Team was having a camp out to bond for the upcoming season. They all got a bit of the munchies and went walking around to find food. They stumbled into the wrong camp. My dad kicked that kids ass. I started laughing because after my dad took him down two other players emerged from the trees stoned out of their minds like "bro chill, we are just looking for a snack, no harm."

Well sneaking into a camp with three teenage girls was a bad plan bro. My little sister was mortified. She thought that the guys would remember her and she would be tagged as the girl with the crazy dad. None of the guys remembered shit from that night. God knows how they even made it though the night. They all had to be wreaked the next day. A couple months later I saw them at Cunha's Country Store getting a sandwich, they had no clue whom I was. I just laughed to myself and went on my way.

We all shared a story or two that night. Boomer kept poking at me to come shooting with them. I agreed to it knowing I would never see them again.

Me: "I know after we go shooting you will never want to see me again so might as well get it over with."

Boomer: "What the hell does that mean?"

Me as the second beer hit me: "Because I can shoot better than all of you put together. You have no idea what it is like to be raised by a man with three daughters"

Kid: "I may want to meet your dad sooner than later"

The night was so nice. I really did not want it to end. The guys were staying at Kihei Kai Oceanfront Condos so they called for an Uber and we waited out front. When the driver arrived I gave them all a big hug goodbye. Turbo was the last to get in the van. He gave me a kiss on the cheek, smiled and got in the van. They drove away leaving me standing in the parking lot stunned. For the first time in my life I lost track of time and space. I jolted moments later not realizing I totally spaced out. That Eric gave me a kiss. And I liked it.

The next morning my phone started buzzing like crazy. I had no clue who was trying do get a hold of me. It was a missed call from a number I did not know and a text message. Actually a couple from the same number:

Wake up. We are hungry. Where should we meet?

Hello?

It's Eric BTW

Reading the last text jolted me out of bed. I slept in longer than I usually do. I think it was the beers. I can't even remember drinking that much beer before. Grosse. I felt bad but breakfast was a great idea. So I text back:

Kihei Caffe

Immediately I got back:

See you in 20

What twenty minuets? Are you serious? Thankfully I showered last night so getting ready wouldn't take that long. I wondered how long they have been up? This must be second nature for them to drink all night and get up totally functional. I got myself together looking like a normal girl. Bikini, cut off denim shorts and a tank. Of course I had to take my cross body bag. Nothing too big, just a bag large enough for some money and a couple safety necessities to side on the error of caution; I had to look like a normal young woman.

I jumped into my dad's jeep and drove down the road to meet the guys. When I got there they were already waiting for me. I know I didn't take longer than twenty minuets but I guess these guys need to eat. They were already in line, which was a good call. It is a popular spot, especially during the tourist season. Luckily today wasn't too bad, there were places to sit along with it not being too hot out. For some reason, even after coming here every year since I was little I still find the humidity to get to me every now and then. I blame living in the Bay Area.

I order the French toast like always do, with all the add-on's which include macadamia nuts and coconut syrup. It is so good. I know it will heal my beer battered tummy. I get a Cappuccino and water too. I need to start hydrating. The guys are stoked about the menu and we find a picnic bench out front. The weather provides a nice breeze and everything seems is calm. The guys talk about stuff happening on base, they are going on and on about how Richard has been on a rampage trying to get answers. They talk like I am clued into what they are saying. They may have forgotten I am even there, well all but one of them. Regardless I need to check in on Richard's findings later. Not realizing it I catch Eric looking at me. I smile not sure of what to do and he smiles back. I am so ackward.

Our food comes and we all dive in. The conversation turns to their plans to relax at the beach until their flight leaves later today and the heavy carbohydrates soak up the leftover alcohol left inside. That news of them leaving makes me sad but I knew they were only here for the shaved ice. We finish up, talk some more and head to the parking lot. As we walk Eric asks me my plans for lunch. Not thinking it through I blurt out after a giggle Paia Fish Market as it is my new favorite spot on the island and it is right next to the café we just ate. He laughs too then all of a sudden he yells to the guys he is going to stay back and will catch up with them later. Standing next to the door to my jeep, I look at him as if I do not know what is happening and he gets in the passenger seat. He looks over at me and says, "So what do you want to do until lunch?"

I smile and just get into the jeep while my inner school girl is doing backflips that this hot guy is ditching his friends to spend time with me. I am totally lost but am skilled in the art of staying calm and thinking on my feet.

Eric: "What do you like to do when you visit your dad?" I just start the engine and drive. We head back to my dads place and get the paddleboards. I think it might be funny to see this strong guy try his hand at some balance on the open ocean.

We make our way out to the waves and I warn him the area we will be going over tends to be a shark friendly area. He laughs but I know he is trying to figure out if I am joking or not. We head south. After last night I don't know how long I will last but it is a nice activity. Just jump in the water to cool off and keep going. I did bring two waters just in case we need to hydrate. The day is perfect. There is a light breeze and not too many people on the beach. I catch Eric /checking everything out. It doesn't get better than this. Luckily the wind is not too strong this morning and we are able to do a lap up and down the coast.

We make our way back after a couple hours. Eric is bright red. I may be should have recommended some sunscreen but him being a full grown adult I guess I didn't think I had to suggest it. We rinse off at the outside shower and I realize he is wearing his silkies. I think they are Marines safety blankets. I called them Marine Panties to my childhood friend once and he did not like that. It still makes me laugh thinking about it and his reaction. I just kept saying it as get kept trying to correct me until he finally gave up. Eric catches me smirking at him and he smiles back.

Though we just ate we are both hungry so we head out for lunch. Instead of going back toward the cafe I decided to drive us up to the original location, in Paia. It is a cute little street we can walk around. Once we find parking we head to get lunch and window shop on our way.

Once we sit I realize how easy it is to talk to Eric. I am not so good with people and small talk, but with Eric I am able to have a nice conversation. We compare notes about growing up with Marine parents. We have very different experiences. His mother and father where very concerned with letting him experience school, social engagements, sports and other things. My dad was concerned with self-defense and gun safety. Eric got a bit of that too but nothing in comparison to my crash course in how to murder and walk away without a trace.

After we eat we walk around and take in the sites. I make him do more than window shop though. He wasn't too thrilled about going into the actual stores at first but I felt since I was here I may as well pick up some things for Danielle and the upcoming Maid of Honor requirements she had listed for me. I had to laugh. What is it about guys and shopping? In one store there is a guy behind the counter trying not to be in your face customer service. As we are looking around he asks, "Are you looking to get your girl friend any thing in particular?"

I froze. I guess it is an honest mistake but I did not know what to say or do. The last twenty-four hours have been so foreign to me socially. Eric was flawless in his response and casually said "No we are just looking. Thanks." Totally smooth.

After that we headed back to the jeep. I figured we could head up to Makawao before having to get him to his flight on time. I really do not know how to be tour guide but I figure I will take him to the places I like. Not like we are going to see each other again. If he doesn't have fun at least I enjoyed myself.

Makawao is funky. It is a small street on the side of the mountain. When we get there it is raining so we duck into the blown glass shop. When I was little my dad would bring me up here and we would sit for hours and watch the artist make new items. Eric really liked it.

When the rain stopped we walked the town. Got a snack and found a bench to people watch. Sitting there not looking at each other Eric speaks up and asks: "Did you like what you saw back at the outdoor shower?"

Me: "I'm not sure how to answer that"

Eric: "You seemed to enjoy watching me rinse off in my silkies. I thought you might have gotten an eye full of something you liked."

Me: "I enjoy looking at you if that's what your asking"

Eric: "Ok, I will take that. What was the giggle about then?"

So me being totally out of my element and not prepared for these personal questions about myself and or my feelings for that matter blurt out: "You are wearing Marine Panties." And then I started to giggle again. Laughing hard with me at this point, Eric takes a couple deep breaths and asks me what the hell I was talking about. So I explain to him my conversation with my childhood friend and how silkies are essentially Marine Panties. Laughing still he tries to explain they are tactical clothing but we are both laughing too hard to really care at this point. It was a nice moment. I felt relaxed like I usually do with Danielle. Danielle and I can laugh about nothing for hours so it was nice to have a moment with someone else like this. Made me feel normal for a minuet.

On the drive back to Kihei he asked if I could just take him to the airport to meet the guys. I guess time passed a little faster than I realized. We arrived a little early so we hung in the cell phone lot for a bit.

Eric: "Can I call you?"

Me: "I'd like that"

Eric: "Will you come see me before you head home?"

Me hesitating: "Sure"

Then before I realized what was going on he leaned in and kissed me. Not on the cheek but a real kiss. I am not sure how long it lasted but I giggled when he finally pulled away. He liked it too and I could tell he was nervous about it. Then he did it again. When his phone started to buzz I knew our time was up. We both just smiled at each other and we just drove in silence to drop him off.

At the curb the guys where waiting for him with big stupid smiles. Man I knew he was going to get a ration of shit for ditching them today and I could tell by their faces they knew we must have kissed or something. I think it was easy to tell we liked each other or at least he liked me. He hadn't taken his eyes off me since meeting. Before getting out he leaned in again and gave me one last kiss goodbye. The guys went wild and I started to laugh.

Me: "Bye guys! Have a safe jump."

The Guys: "Bye Guava"

Eric: "See you later"

So now I am Guava.

Getting Serious?

The rest of the day I was just stupid. I attempted to do some work when I got back to my dads but then headed down to the beach because I could not concentrate. I just sat in my lounge chair and watched the waves. I was totally zoned out. Though it was nice to really relax, I felt a little off, like I was not in control and it really made me dizzy. Here at my spot I am aware of my surrounding but I can do nothing. I do not have to think about work. Nothing matters. In my dazed moment trying to figure out what the last twenty-four hours were about I hear my phone buzz.

I had a great day today. Wish I could have stayed longer.
Me: *Next time we will go snorkeling.* ☺
I can't wait to see you again
Me: *Same*
Can you come see me before you leave?
Me: *I think so. Just waiting to hear from my dad*
Bring him too. I'm sure the guys would love to met him
Me: *Are you just using me to get to my awesome Marine dad?*
NO way. Come now and I will prove it too you. ☺

How do I flirt? Is he flirting or being nice? Man, this is one thing I know nothing about. I feel like I need to get Danielle on board to guide me through the dos and don'ts. As I contemplate my response I get a call. It was dad. He is in Oahu and asked me to come over to see him so I tell him about my new friends and he is actually excited to meet them. What did I just do? I am having my dad meet the men I saved, stalked and now one I like, one being possibly borderline boyfriend. I should have taken up drinking. The mission, the guys and now the past day are still spinning in my head when my phone pings again.

Hello?

Me: *Dad just called. Ill be over the day after tomorrow*

Really? I can't wait

Me: *I'm booking my flight and room as we speak*

Where are you staying?

Me: *Recommendations?*

Google it. Not sure what accommodations you like

Me: (thumbs up)

Me: *I can stay near you at Paradise Bay Resort or Get real fancy and stay in Waialae......what you think?*

Dunno

Me: *Want do fancy with me? After all I am on vacation*

I'd love too. But I get to take you around this time

Me: *Deal*

It's a date!

If that's okay with you, that we date

Me: *It's a date*

Let me know when you get checked in and I will head your way

Me: *See you in a couple days*

I can't wait

I did not divulge the entire story to dad over the phone. I am sure he is just glad I made some friends. There were a couple guys back home in High School he would always ask me about. Like he really wanted to marry me off at the same time he is teaching me to take peoples lives. It was too much for me as a teenager to absorb. So I learned to kill. I am still, friendly with those guys on Facebook, they are both married and their wives are the sweetest. There is no way I could have offered them what they needed. These women are impeccable, they cook, clean, watch the kids. All I have to offer is how to kill and not get caught. May be single life is best for me.

I fly in around noon and my dad will pick me up. He will debrief me over lunch and then drop me off. He is finishing up an assignment and will be taking his new lady friend camping. She still works so he takes assignments and sees her in between. God knows where he stays. I should have known by the lack of food at the condo dad hasn't been home for a while. Not sure if it is because of this new woman or if he has been taking more assignments. I sure hope it is because of his new girlfriend. I really like her and she seems to navigate things like my mom did. She is a good balance for him.

I pass the time before my vacation trip by getting some Maid of Honor duties done. I text and email Danielle what I have come up with and she loves it all. Danielle sends me over my dress options and I am not completely frightened. I am getting excited for her wedding. I may even have a date. I package up the items Eric helped me get in Paia and have it ready to drop off at the post office before I hit the airport.

I pack a bag for my dad like he asked and get my stuff ready to go. I go into town and get the bridesmaid baskets made and sent with the extra goodies I got in Paia. Danielle wants Kona coffee, macadamia nuts and little champagne's mailed to each Bridesmaid as her "Will you be my Bridesmaid?" She will pay me back. She has picked Blue as her wedding color. They will be getting married at Our Lady of the Pillar in Half Moon Bay and the reception is going to be at Mezza Luna. Her and Matt cannot agree on a place to have the rehearsal dinner. I recommended the Moss Beach Distillery. My sister had hers there and it was good. Matt wants Barbra's Fishtrap and Danielle wants Pasta Moon. No matter where they pick it will be good food. The nice thing about Half Moon Bay is the seafood and the restaurants are all delicious.

I am getting kind of nervous as the time to leave creeps up on me. I do not know why I am so anxious about going to see the guys. I know I will be spending more time with Eric, and alone time at that. I am surprised my dad has a TV but I am thankful to switch it on and try and forget about tomorrow. I am really stressing over nothing. I find some home renovation show and get totally immersed in the before and after.

My dad picks me up at the airport and we head to eat. We hit a food truck in the park for lunch and go over my last mission. He is surprised I had to wait as long as I did and is also happy about my actions with the Marines. When I informed him they are the same group of guys I met at Ululani's he reacts with a scowl and gets quiet.

My dad understands my actions and how everything was resolved but he is not happy how I am currently involved. He is old fashion and once a job is complete it is over. You walk away and never look back. I told him about Richard and the false Intel which diverts my guilt and he decided he would make some inquires about it too. My dad actually knows Richard from back in his Marine Days. I didn't realize Richard was that old? After my dad hears everything he needs we head to my luxury accommodations. We take the H3 to the 63 to the 83. Dad makes fun of me for reserving such a nice place to stay. I told him I have to keep up appearances for work and may be land them as a client. I am supposed to be a successful marketing manager for start up companies and businesses looking to enter into new markets after all. He just laughs at me.

I think he forgets that we once stayed at Le Royal in Dubai. It was wonderful and we were in full Marketing family trip cover back then. My dad told us his client was hosting us to better help him with the direction they should take for potential clients. Really dad and I were there to kill four tourist trying to purchase young kids and transport them to Europe.

I drop off my stuff and dad informs me to hurry up because we have to get to the base. Reading my confusion he explains that he has scheduled a tour with Richard and the guys. Apparently since mom died he has been in close contact with the base and some of his old pals. He also knew more about the guys than he made out, or he did his research last night after our talk. Thanks Dad, he always has to one up me on everything.

We move through security with ease. Dad seems to know everyone. Not that it is much of a surprise. With what we do its better to know all parties involved. My dad was a Marine (and will always be a Marine). I guess it never goes away. I wonder if I can have a life outside of killing. My dad had a spouse and family. May be one day I can have it too. I never really thought about it before. It would be a balancing act for sure. I am not sure if my dad ever told my mom who he really was and this didn't sit well with me. I want to be able to have that conversation with someone. I want them to know who I truly am. I don't want them to fear me in any way but fully accept me for all that I am. It is a big ask, and I know it is just fairy tale stuff but its what I want. I may be setting myself up for failure but I deserve to shoot for the stars.

The guys and Richard are all waiting for us at the shooting range. They have an assortment of weapons laid out. I am glad I wore leggings, a tank and a Giants hat on the plane. A sundress is not the best shooting attire. I felt as if my dad may have set this all up on purpose. What did he know that I did not? The guys are happy to see me and call out when I get out of the jeep.

Boomer: "Hey Guava, you ready to show off your skills?"

Me: "Are you ready to get your ass handed to you?"

The guys laugh as my dad walks up and introductions are made. Richard calls my dad Sir so the guys follow suit.

Sir: "You guys get ready, my daughter is going to show you pussy pansey asses proper form. You new breed of Marines are soft."

Richard: "God only knows you trained your daughter to be a skilled killer. I would not expect anything less old man."

I smile. If only he knew that is exactly what Sir did. The guys are in awe of my dad. He has seen war and faced many interesting situations. I guess Richard has debriefed them. Richard motions to me and says "Ladies First." My dad just smiles and nods at me. He is giving me the okay to show my skills. Dad is usually reserved but I think he may be hoping I scare these guys away.

I look over the selection, then at the target. I estimate the distance and do the numbers in my head. I find a comfortable pair of earmuffs and make my first selection. I had not noticed but everyone was silent and watching my every move. Eric looked curious. He gave me a hug and kiss on the cheek when I arrived but was mostly engaged in conversation with my dad up until now. They all really wanted to see if the stories where true and if I was just all talk.

I get into position with the M500A2 Shotgun. It is a 12-Gauge shotgun that usually comes with a five-round capacity tube. After I fire off a couple shots I turn around to see my dad with the biggest smirk and all the guys stunned. I smile and ask: "Does anyone else want to try?"

The guys finally move and Boomer turned to Eric to say: "Good luck Buddy. And don't even try to mess with that one. She will put you out to pasture if you step out of line." The comment doesn't faze him, Eric walks past me and whispers "I think I may love you now" and picks up his gun and we go back to shooting.

It was a fun couple of hours but Dad, Sir and Richard ended up on the conversation of the false Intel and they decide to hit the office to do some research. My dad tells me to take off with Eric and he will catch up with me later. This surprises me because I guess I always thought my dad would be over protective with me dating. I am assuming the last hour proved that I am okay on my own.

Eric grabs his bag and we head to the hotel. We hit the beach. We talk about random stuff. He grills me about Danielle's wedding. I guess the guys were all at the Kids wedding and it was a blast. I am trying to figure out the details of the Bachelorette party still and he has about a million suggestions. Since we grew up on Half Moon Bay and still live there, the guest list is going to be long. I know a couple girls that will fly in for the event so I want to make sure it is worth it and prove to some of them I am the best Maid of Honor ever. Danielle's cousin will be in charge of the Shower, I am glad I do not have to plan everything. Her cousin Angela is great and I know will do a killer job. Angela grew up with us and in the same neighborhood as Danielle. For a while we were all really close in High School. Then life happens and we went our own ways. We are still all friends though.

Sir swings by to have dinner with us and grabs his bag I packed him. He will be gone for a couple weeks camping but I know what he is really up too. I know he will call when he is finished just to check in and recap anything I may be up to or any other assignments I may take until then. And if I do not hear from him at the scheduled time I know the protocol for the following seventy-two hours, then the following week. Sir and Eric get along smoothly. They talk shop at dinner. I zone in and out of the conversation, check my surroundings, and watch the people. I notice a couple tables down there are a cute family. The parents are both on their phones, the kids on tablets no one engaging one another. What is the point of even going out to dinner might as well stay home. I promise myself if I ever have kids that will not be me.

Sir takes off and we head back to the room. The resort is a lot nicer than expected. There is an awkward silence of what to do next. I know we planned for him to stay with me to hang but we never really talked about anything else. I flash that this may be the moment we start getting hot and heavy and I get a little uneasy because I really did not pack anything sexy to wear to bed. I really should have called Danielle. I have no idea how to proceed so I just say, "I guess I'll jump in the shower."

My shower is uneventful. I was expecting some Danielle Steele romance scene where Eric comes in and helps me clean up. Nothing happened. I dry off, wrap a towel around me and walk into the bedroom. Eric is gone. As weird as that is I am not surprised. Though my sexual encounters have been minimal I really thought he liked me. May be he is being a good guy. I really know nothing of these situations and cannot read into them because it is an unknown territory. My last partner was this nice guy in college, purely sexual. We acknowledged each other in passing but there was no dates, spending time together or making out. It was a hand shake agreement we made one night when we got locked out of our dorm rooms while our room mates got it on with random people.

Half way through putting my clothes on (just under ware at this point. Should have hit up Victoria's before I came) Eric enters the room. There is an odd pause then "Hey, sorry I realized we had nothing to drink so I went to get some waters and snacks."

Me: "Thanks"

I notice he doesn't take his eyes off me and is totally still. I move to grab the ice bucket and say "Guess Ill go get some ice."

Eric: "Like that?"

My bad. I am frozen. About a foot away from him I look down at myself and start to laugh. "I guess I should put something on."

Eric: "okay?"

He puts down the bag of drinks and heads to the bathroom. Perplexed I put the bucket down and sit on the only bed in the room to text Danielle. I definitely need some help navigating this. Waiting for Danielle's response I look at my email, check social media then notice that Eric is standing in front of me in only a towel. "Did you go get ice in that?"

Me: "Oh no. I spaced it. I had to finish a work thing."

Eric: "Is that what you sleep in?"

Me: "Sometimes?"

Eric: "Okay"

Me: "Okay"

Eric: "I'll get ice right now then."

He grabs the ice bucket and heads out the room, in just his towel. He gets back and I guess I am just sitting there staring at him and looking confused.

Eric: "What's wrong?"

Me: "Funny you just went to get the ice in a towel but you questioned me to go in my under ware?"

Eric: "I didn't want anyone to see you like that."

Me: "But its okay if people see you like that?"

Eric: "Is it okay if people see me like this?"

I just smile because I really don't know what this is. Is he flirting? We have kissed, gone shooting with my dad, he said he loved me jokingly and we just took showers not together but in the same room and now we are going to sleep in the same bed. I really should start watching more movies. He smiles back, puts on some boxers and pulls out a bottle of wine from the bag.

We sit on the bed drinking wine and flipping through the channels until we find Goonies. It's a classic so we agree to watch it. Sitting close together in bed, not saying anything is somewhat intense. We polish off the bottle during the movie and Ghostbusters comes on. We don't speak but start sinking deeper into the bed as we just watch TV.

We both wake up in the morning cuddling. I decide to just go with it. I like him and if he likes me it will all work out. If not I just go back to my life. I made an oath after graduating High School when my basic training was over and college I would start my assignments. I knew dad would ease me into each assignment testing my skills. Needless to say I advanced quickly. My year abroad in France was so much fun in many ways. The food, people and community were so different than the bay area. I loved school and the assignments were equally fun. But there was no room for romance. All work and no play.

My assignments consisted of luring men into dark allies and making them disappear. I found if I dressed and acted a certain way it was actually quite easy. Most of my marks where young up and coming men in the crime world, they where looking to party and flash their money. It was easy pickings. I gained the skill of flirtation but observation but it was all an act. Being invisible made it easy for me to observe and gain information about each of them. Makeup made it easy to look however I wanted. Some times I would draw it out over two nights to make it interesting. Never once did they recognize me. Even the bouncers at the nightclubs and bar tenders did not remember me. I would see them out and about in the town and they would walk right by me. It was almost too easy.

I realized fast that once I got the men alone they wanted to go zero to sixty as fast as they could. I know most of them where accustomed to paid sex so I had to play whatever part I was playing. There was never more than kissing involved, mostly in public to keep up appearances. I would always feel dirty after and slowly stopped using that method. I know since they all left with me quite easy I was attractive.

I hope Eric thought so too, being that I am bare bones now, no makeup and in my under garments. I hope I am not just the friend. But if so it would not be the first time. I wanted him to really want me. I didn't know what to do or what my next move should be. He was obvious in some of the things he said but for some reason I could not process what he was saying. I just could not grasp that it was me he was seeing and wanting. I knew then that I really was out of touch with human relationships.

I got up to brush my teeth and Eric moved a little. Eric joined me in my morning routine, both not saying a word. As I turned to leave the bathroom he caught my arm, pulled me into him and gave me a kiss. We continued to kiss. I am not sure how long we stayed in the bathroom and made out but we only stopped because there was a knock at the door.

Eric had ordered us breakfast the night before and arranged it to be delivered at a specific time. He ordered me the loaded waffles and coffee. It is like he knows me. We shared the red seasoned potatoes and bacon. Half way through the meal Eric said "The timing couldn't have been worse but I hope you like it."

Me: "I love it. I didn't realize how hungry I was."

Eric: "Must have been the wine last night?"

Me: "We didn't drink that much but seemed to pass out never the less."

Eric: "You passed out first. I almost took it offensively."

Me: "I fell asleep first? That never happens."

I guess I trusted the guy. I never do that. This made me uneasy. For a split second I contemplated him being hired to target me. He was attentive and observant. Was he too attentive? Too observant? I think I started to get slightly paranoid at this point.

Me: "Why would you be offended? Did I snore?"

Eric after his large laugh: "No but I have never had a girl fall asleep on me before."

Me: "Oh, Sorry. I am not used to having company."

Eric: "I didn't mean it like that. I don't spend time with a lot of women, or any women at that. I haven't had a girl friend since before my first mission."

Me: "Okay"

Eric: "I have been with women just not anything serious. I don't want you to think I am, actually I am making myself sound terrible."

Me: "You don't have to tell me anything."

Eric: "Why not?"

Me: "Well we just met, and your past is your past. If you want me in your future you will make it happen. I guess."

Eric: "Your right."

Me: "Okay"

Eric: "So do you have a boyfriend?"

Me: "I wouldn't be kissing you if I had one."

Eric: "Good to know."

Me: "Do you have a girlfriend?"

Eric: "Not yet."

After breakfast we spent the day paddle boarding, hitting the beach and lounging around. We headed back to the room late afternoon to shower before dinner. He had something planned. We dressed casual. He wore shorts over his silkies, a button up shirt and some vans so I opted for a sundress and sandals not knowing what was in store I wanted to look good for him. He asked me where I put the jeep keys. He had given them to me when we got here after the base so I told him to look in the side pocket of my purse. Walking out of the bathroom looking for my lip gloss I had not anticipated what was to come next. Eric looked up at me with such confusion I knew exactly what he had found in my bag.

Me: " I have been caring one since I was in college. Per my dad."

My heart is racing, I hope I haven't blown my cover. I am in total inner turmoil that he has figured out who I am. What lasted only one second felt like minuets and I was worried. I had never had these feeling before and this was starting to really fuck with me mentally.

Eric: "I get it."

Me: "Are you okay with it?"

Eric: "Yeah, sorry I really don't know why it surprised me."

Me trying to make light of the situation: "Don't worry, Ill protect you."

Eric still stunned: "I guess you will."

Me: "Do you want to carry it?"

Eric looking surprised I asked immediately responded: "No"

Me: "I could leave it if you prefer?"

Eric: "No way, then you will feel uncomfortable. I know the feeling."

Me: "I have another in my luggage if you want to carry one too."

After a heavy laugh, Eric is finally relaxed about finding a Gloc in my bag and says, "No that's fine. I guess I just never met someone so much like me. I never thought I would be dating a girl that could kill me at any moment."

Me: "Guess you better treat me good then."

Eric: "Always. And not because I might be physically harmed."

Me: "Then lets go. I want to know my surprise."

Eric drove us to a nice restaurant. I guess his parents took him here the first time they visited and he liked it. It was pretty, totally Aloha. The restaurant sat us in our own little corner with a great view. After a couple minuets looking over the menu Eric ordered a Crown and Coke and I ordered a Grey Goose and seven. Guess this is a real date after all.

When the waitress brought the drinks over she rattled off the specials and they all sounded so good. I asked Eric if he wanted to split the coconut shrimp with me to be polite though I secretly wanted it all to myself. He decided we should order the meal and split it but also order our own entrees as well. I opted for the filet and veggies and he went with the ribs and garlic mash potatoes. Dinner was excellent. We ate everything and event taste tested each other's as well.

We walked slowly to our room after dinner absolutely in no hurry. The elevator was fun. I didn't want it to stop. I really didn't know what was suppose to happen next so I decided to let Eric make the moves. I was worried if I was to forward I might ruin the mood. Once we got into our room Eric checked his phone to find five missed calls from Boomer, asking me politely first then calling him right back and walked onto the balcony. I flipped on the TV and waited, it must have been something important for him to stop what we were doing, and about to do. I was relieved but bummed at the same time. Something about Eric made me want this to be special.

Eric came in and started talking a mile a minuet and I knew our smoochy time was for sure, over. Richard had come across information that someone had purposely composed their twenty-five Marine team and sent them to me weeks ago. Boomer feels that some how all twenty-five guys are connected with a common denominator and Eric suggested similar missions with the same target. At that Boomer wanted to get with Richard and try and run down some leads.

I know this is big news for the guys and finding out their mission was a bust and a set up makes me start to think about my own assignment. I am glad they are getting somewhere and I know Sir has some questions about it all he is getting answers for as well. Sadly that also means there is someone feeding the Marine Corp false Intel. That is a major breech and I make a mental note to follow up with Sir once I get home. Eric only has a couple more days of leave before he has to report back to base but I think he may be heading back sooner than later. This lead has all the guys wondering.

The Kid is having a family barbeque tomorrow and we are all invited, especially me. Apparently I am the hot social topic of the group and I will be able to get a read on the Eric and I situation and see where Eric and I stand after that. He comes and sits next to me in bed and we watch TV. It is comfortable. It is nice. I hope he enjoys it as much as I do. Not to be selfish but I really don't want it to end.

Everyone arrives early for the barbeque. These guys run on the same clock. They are in the back yard when we get there so I let Eric go chat and offer my help to the Kids wife. She looks like she is going to pop any second. I am surprised she is moving around the kitchen so fast. By the looks of her legs I would think she would want to be laying down. She starts calling out commands and I step into my role making the guacamole when I look up and see Eric staring at me.

Me with a smirk: "What is it?"

Eric: "After finding your weapon it is nice to know you can be domestic too."

Me: "You like your women barefoot in the kitchen?"

Eric: "I think I would like you any way possible."

Smiling at me I feel my cheeks getting hot. His comment brings me back to the elevator last night before Boomers call, I am going to take it as a sign he wants me. I don't know how the next days will play out but I am hoping it goes past just kissing. I am really out of my element but I just go with it at this point. Knowing he made me blush he walks over and sticks his finger in my guacamole bowl and tries my recipe.

Eric: "Not bad. I guess I will keep you."

Me: "What makes you think you have me yet?"

Eric: "Is that a challenge?"

Me: "Lets see what you got."

And in once swift move he pushed the bowl out of my hands and had me pinned against the counter. No one has ever had the upper hand on me before. I was mad at myself at the same time totally aroused. I am having a really hard time getting myself in check these last couple of days.

Eric: "Can you handle?"

Me trying to play tough: "Give me what you got."

The Kid and Boomer walked in moments later as we are in full make out mode in the kitchen with me sitting on the counter next to my guacamole. The Kid cleared his throat to let us know they were in the kitchen being that he is a gentleman and has the best manners. Eric turned around to them and calmly asked what they needed as if there was nothing going on. Boomer just boomed with laughter.

Boomer: "Damn Guava!"

Eric: "Shut up Boomer"

Kid: "We just came in to get the meat to put on the grill."

Boomer: "Looks like Guava is getting Turbo's meat ready."

Totally embarrassed, my cheeks had to be bright red and wanting to hide I realize for the first time I am not invisible and I am not a fan of being the center of attention either.

Eric: "Don't be jealous she thinks I'm better looking than you. I know that is a blow to your ego."

Boomer: "I'm not going to mess with her dude. She is gentle, sexy, but deadly as hell. I saw the way she shot the other day. She could kill us all and no one would ever expect it to be her."

After they leave Eric looks down at me and says: "You know I believe him but I am not scared."

Me concerned and not following: "What do you mean?"

Eric: "I think you can do things I do not want to know about. But I am okay with it."

Me thinking he knows: "You are?"

Eric: "Yeah. I know you would never hurt me."

The table and food was set. We all sat at the long kitchen picnic table outside. A couple of the other guys from base joined us as well. I guess the Kid and his wife Elle have people over a lot. They like to make sure the guys have a sense of family. And all these guys have become a close family and it shows the way they interact with each other. It is nice to be apart of it in this moment. As people are passing around plates Elle turns to me and asks, "Logan says you are quite the shot. It has been quite the topic the last day or so. I know how we will be raising our daughters now."

Me shaking my head and looking down: "I'm okay."

Boomer: "You are more than okay. You could kills us all now without batting an eye."

Eric: "Your dad made sure you would always be safe."

Boomer: "Guess she doesn't need you."

Me with a smirk and out of know where: "Well for some things."

The conversation goes into my skill. The other men at the table ask me questions about my dad and my training. No one could believe my dad just wanted us girls to be safe. It was fun to talk about my dad making us all clean his guns Saturday morning before we could go play or out with our friends. Doc's wife Madison shared stories of Doc teaching his kids similar things but in less extreme ways. I know I have certain skills that most women do not but I hope I did not give myself away. Sir promoted me showing off so in the end I will blame him if my cover is blown.

As conversation progressed I learned that Elle has patched up many soldier's and has experienced a lot of the bad that goes with war and the special forces. When getting pregnant the first time she decided to get out of the emergency arena and into the day-to-day hospital stuff. She now works for a local doctor in an office and likes coming home only having to deal with day-to-day colds and not full on amputations.

I did not know how long I was memorized by the dynamic of the group. I went into people watching coma after I finished my hamburger when Eric squeezed my thigh and brought me back to reality.

Eric whispering in my ear: "You okay?"

Me: "Yeah, this is nice. Thank you for inviting me."

Eric: "I like having you as my plus one."

Me: "Me too"

Eric: "Want to keep going?"

Me: "Yes"

Boomer breaking us out of our little hushed back and forth: "So what have you two lovers been doing since we say you last?"

Elle: "Yeah how long have you been together? Sorry I have not been briefed in on what is happening in every ones social life. The mystery of the guys last mission has been all any one ever talks about."

Eric: "We just started dating"

Me: "Yeah we met in Maui."

Elle: "I love Maui, though I think the big island if my favorite."

Doc: "No Kaui had to be the best. More to do."

Boomer: "There is one and only Oahu."

Dad: "I prefer the mainland so all of you shut up."

With Dads comment the whole table burst into a heated discussion. There were arguments over arguments, battle of the islands. I had to laugh. In the mix of all the chaos Eric leans down to me and whispers; "Want to be my girl friend?"

Me: "Yes"

And with that, no one else mattered. We just started to kiss. With Eric I felt relaxed and for the first time I spaced out and enjoyed my surroundings. I wasn't worried about my escape route or my evacuation plan. I soaked it in and absorbed the moment. I felt comfortable with him in a way I did not have to explain myself. I don't have to tell him but I am not hiding it from him either. It was new to me, uncomfortable but I like it. I think Volbeat's I only want to be with you was playing on the radio. I would remember this moment forever.

Boomer: "You guys done? There are kids present."

Eric: "Guess its time for them to learn where they came from."

Boomer concerned: "Be good to him Guava. Just be good to him."

Me: "Will do"

So for the first time in my life I have a real boyfriend. I may be older than most but at least I am not the forty year old virgin. I know Danielle is going to flip out. When Eric was in the shower I had to finally call her back. She blew up my phone. I had to describe his every physical feature in grave detail. Danielle was so excited for me but entirely disappointed we haven't done the nasty yet. She told me to wrap it up and make him mine already, seal the deal. Danielle thinks sex solves everything but I think I am off to a good start.

Mission

I was actually got really sad when it was time to leave. Eric ended up getting totally drunk at the barbeque so getting him back to the room was a little difficult. Boomer and Dad helped me get him into the jeep but the jeep butgetting to our room was a challenge. I am strong for my size but he is about a foot taller than me and about a hundred pounds heavier. I left him passed out in the chair all night after his shower. I am thankful he was even able to shower at all I got nervous thinking he might crash through the glass. After getting him in the chair I showered and went to bed. The next morning was funny. He was hurting bad. We ended up just relaxing in bed and watching movies. It was something neither of us had ever done.

Eric did not start to feel normal until around dinner. Sadly it was time for him to head back. After it took him thirty minuets to actually leave. He apologized for drinking so much and not spending more time with me when we got back to the room. I think he was sad he got too drunk and couldn't do it like Danielle had said five times on the phone last night. I don't want my first time with him to be a drunken disaster that he doesn't remember, plus what do I get out of it if he is a complete mess? After he goes I finalized my bachelorette party plans and ordered the invites.

Is it bad I miss you already?

Me: *No*

I didn't want to stop kissing you. It's going to be hard being away from you

Me: *Distance makes the heart grow fonder*

That's not all

Me: *(shy emoji)*

When I get home I start laundry, shower and head down to the dungeon. Losing track of time I keep myself busy. I hate the red eye flights back from Hawaii. I feel like that is all they offer any more and it takes a day just to recover from that. Around the same time I head up to rotate the laundry I hear banging on my front door. Who the hell? Danielle. She comes right in and plops down on my couch.

Danielle: "Tell me everything.

Me: "Well he asked me to be his girlfriend at the barbeque then got drunk so we just slept that night. You already know this."

Danielle: "And?"

Me: "I told you everything else when I called you. We kissed a lot before he left and he text me as soon as he got back to base."

Danielle: "When are you going to see him again?"

Me: "Not sure. I didn't ask."

Danielle: "Is he on Facebook? You are bringing him to my wedding right?"

Me: "I did mention needing a plus one."

Danielle: "He is your date. I already put him down. Is he going to fly out for the Bachelorette?"

Me: "No. Why would he?"

Danielle: "To see you of course. Why not? He can come out and spend the weekend. We have the shower at Angela's parents ranch then he can hang with Matt and the guys the night of the party. It will be great!"

Me: "I don't know. I think he would be cool to chill with Matt but not your brothers and cousin Tim."

Danielle: "OMG Cousin Tim is the best. He makes a total ass of himself every time. What is not to love?"

Me: "Well we just met Danielle. Its all happened so fast, don't you think all this is a lot?"

Danielle: "If its meant to be it is meant to be."

Me: "Fine. I'll ask."

Danielle: "Okay let's go then because I'm hungry. San Benito House for dinner and have some drinks."

Me: "Fine, let me change."

Not realizing it I had not heard from Eric in a day or so. I do not know the protocol but I guess he had to do some work. Just as promised I call and leave a message inviting him to Half Moon Bay the weekend of Danielle's Shower. I would like to see him sooner but with the holidays coming up I bet he will go see his parents. February it may be the soonest we get together. I do not know what to expect but I am hoping that I was not just a weekend romance for him. Though it makes for a good story.

Danielle's wedding is in May and there is so much to do. Her and Matt agreed on Barbra's Fishtrap for the rehearsal dinner. It is a coast side staple. There is a lot here to keep my mind occupied from over analyzing my new relationship and lack of any other relationship in the past to base anything with Eric off of. I guess I will have to take Eric to the Distillery when he comes. I love that place. My phone beeps:

I'm game. Want me to come Thursday through Sunday?

Me: *Yeah that's perfect, Thanks*

Anything for you

Me: (Wink/ Kiss emoji)

Sorry so late, what are your plans for Thanksgiving?

Me taken back: *No worries, I am up. I could go to my sisters but I usually just crash Danielle's Family Dysfunction*

My parents are going to be out of the country. Make me your plus one.

Me: *It's a date*

But Christmas your gonna have to make time for my parents.

Me: *Deal*

Wow. I just made plans with Eric for the holidays. He seems so nonchalant about me asking him to Danielle's and spending the holidays together. I am not sure if this is even real. With that I check in with my dad. I know he does the rounds for the holiday. Splits his time with all three of us. But with his new lady friend I am not sure what he will do. My older sister and her husband usually go on a lavish vacation. They like to visit new places. Summer is for visiting dad. With as hard as they both work they deserve it. I sometimes meet up wit them depending on where dad sends me.

My little sister and her family are chaos. My sister brings her family for the California tour once a year after she visits dad. She hits up family in Napa and makes her way south to Santa Cruz. I send a group text to both of them asking what the plan is. They have their own lives so I understand when we do not always get together. Mom's birthday is when we have been having family time these last couple years.

My older sister and brother-in law text back they will be in Iceland. And my little sister will be with her in-laws. Dad hasn't responded yet. If I do not hear from him by tomorrow I will start to investigate. He hasn't even sent me a new assignment and since I rarely get time off and I just spent a week in Hawaii I know he wouldn't give me more time off.

In the dungeon I get a call on the satellite phone. It can only be dad, or Sir as of late. I answer with "Yes Sir." Dad was not amused and dove right into what he has found out about the Marines mission and his suspicion of it may being linked to my assignment. He has been looking into the guy's past missions. Since he first heard I was there to take out a target and the guys where sent there he has had a feeling something was off. Neither of us has ever encountered a situation like that. Up until then we were myths, ghosts people feared. Sir is thinking someone is trying to connect the dots or track us down. It did not sit well with Sir that my target took so long either.

Most of the myths about us consist of a man no one has ever seen, that takes the lives of the evil people when they least expect it. Most of the countries we travel are Catholic and the guilt of Sin plays a big role in keeping people in line. In some of the Muslim and Jewish populated areas the homeless or street people talk about the Grime Reaper that comes to take your life when he does not agree with your actions. Mostly the bad people disappear so no one really cares. It is the fellow bad people, rapist, murders, and child traffickers, child molesters that are scared. I like it that way.

Sir seems to think the people we are after are connected with Eric's first mission. The blood bath was not the intention of his tour. Eric's mission started out as making rounds, checking in on families and securing the area. It was not a war zone but there had been many issues with it being a passing through spot for drugs and guns. Children would go missing but nothing too concerning, just another populated city with troubled youth. On one of the days a group of Marines went into town and four large trucks made a pit stop for fuel and gas. One of the drivers thought it was a good place to snatch a pretty young girl and relieve some of his stress. Eric and Boomer where the ones who witnessed it and confronted the pervert, ultimately stopping it before it happened and the guy did not like to be told what he could and could not do. Many of these Apparently raping young girls is allowed in his circle of friends. Eric and Boomer managed to free the girl before it got too bad. She was beat up but untouched.

Once the girl was freed, the pervert went ballistic and started to yell and shoot at them. He had a weapon in his boot that neither of them noticed. The few shots the pervert made turned into an all out battle. Boomer called for backup and the marines near by came in attempting to resolve the event. Instead when they arrived, Eric and Boomer where drowning in bullets just barley able to keep the perverts at bay. All the perverts' friends came to join the shooting in a matter of minuets. Not knowing what was in the trucks, it was hard to know where a safe place to shoot was. One of the Marines had taken out all the tires so there could be no escape and this just pissed off one of the perverts even more. The pervert then decided to just blow up the truck. It was caring a large amount of explosives and now someone's bomb supply order had just been canceled. The explosion set the gunfight into overdrive and a building was taken down and one of the other trucks caught fire. It went from rapist to war zone fast.

That day the Marines killed all the transporters and secured the two remaining trucks. The empty truck had been transporting guerrilla soldiers when turned the conformation into a blood bath. One Marine was lost that day. There were countless pedestrians harmed, five dead and all the perverts killed. Eric and Boomer where responsible for most of the kills. The aftermath was hard for Boomer and Eric to absorb but when parents of the girl thanked the young men for saving their daughter they felt they did the right thing. The kills and destruction did not bother Eric and Boomer but how the people lived. They were used to their children being molested and taken. It was the bad in the world that made both men feel like they were drowning. Like there wasn't enough they could ever do to help. It was also the fire inside both of them that pushed them to be better and do more for the world.

Eric and Boomer later that year met with an organization in the United States that helps save children from traffickers and helps them readjust and learn live a normal life. Both men were active in the Charity not only financially but took on roles as pen pals and mentors. Both men may never have children after what they saw. Or they would raise them as I was raised. Eric and I are similar in a way he will never be able to know.

Sir seems to think the organization behind the goods being transported might have set up one of his top ranked guys (the one I was sent to kill) to my given location to see if the Marines, U.S. Government where in fact behind the Ghost killings. Because of the Marines actions that day, there have been false missions/ Intel sent to the U.S. to see if they are apart of the larger picture of so many of the worlds most elite criminals ending up dead over the last fifty years.

Sir tells me that because my kill was made after the guys were already secured it is rumored that the French are helping the Americans. People jump to conclusions so fast and want to blame a person or organization they do not like to begin with just to feel better about it. I have no clue why they chose the French. No one ever thinks that their actions have consequences and it could be someone they have harmed in the past. Who ever it is behind the witch-hunt will end up being hunted himself. Sir tells me it has gone all the way to the top and will be handled immediately. In the hundred and fifty plus years of our organization no one has ever been caught, suspected or even found. I wonder who has that much power and I will never ask. Ignorance is bliss, and it means I can continue to live. I have seen enough movies to know when you start asking questions you end up dead.

Sir tells me I am going to head to Canada for ten days and take in the sights. I plan out my itinerary, pack my bag and head up for bed. My mind is swimming with all the information Sir laid on me. I have a new place in my heart for Eric, Boomer and the boys. I know Canada will be easy and I think Sir knew I could use a light mission after the chaos from the last couple weeks. It will be a cleansing mission, in more ways than one.

Eric calls to fill me in on all that has been happening at the base. The guys are going to be split up into teams of three and sent to different locations around Europe and Africa to get information. The twenty-five Marines got together and shared stories and the common denominator seems to be gun smuggling and human trafficking. They all think there is a bigger player involved and they disrupted some cash flow. There always is someone that calls the shots and in my case when you kill him or her someone steps up into his place. It is a never-ending battle.

Canada goes smoothly as expected. It is easy to move through Canada, no one really cares or sticks their nose in your business. I like no one really asks any questions either, they don't care why you are visiting or what you want to do. I take out half of my targets in the first twenty-four hours. Some of these people are just so predictable. I was disappointed to know that four of my targets are women. Women helping men catch and sell children to be used for God knows what and or pimping out other with just really hits a nerve with me. All my targets are mothers, themselves. Not to have a double standard but I will take my time with them. Sometimes I get into these moods where it feels wrong to let them get away with a bullet to the head, an assisted heart attack or poison. Sometimes I have drawn it out. May be I am messed up too, about to get my period or just a moody woman myself. God will judge me when it is my times. I have come to terms with that.

Two of the women are staying at a shady motel off the freeway. It is almost too easy. Getting into their rooms was nothing. The drug overdose they both had was painful but believable when the police found their bodies a couple days later. The hotel manager noticed and told police they would come and stay while on binges in the past. Their overdose was ruled a standard Heroin overdose. It always works out that way. But those women suffered much more. One even apologized right before she died. For being Plane Jane I always see fear in the eyes of the people I kill and they never expect to me to be the one delivering the punishment.

Making my way across Canada I hit some of my favorite spots. I hope one day I can visit the world with Eric and enjoy the little things. I know I am getting a head of myself thinking of my future with Eric. I just haven't had a boyfriend before and these little fantasies seem the like the adult version of writing his name on a school binder. It would be nice to visit a place and not kill anyone, just a world tour of food, art, architecture and the land. It may be a little far fetched but I have always like Disney movies and I believe there can be a happy ending for me.

My last kills are drawn out as previously stated. I should have known since the first night was so easy the last bunch would take longer. It always works out that way. Like Disneyland, you can ride Indian Jones five times in a row right at eight in the morning when they open, then when you go back after lunch the line is an hour long. I have Disney on the mind because Eric and I talked about it last night while he was finishing up at base and called me to tell me our Christmas plans. I guess his parents are going to be in San Louis Obispo visiting family for Christmas so I will be meeting, not only his parents but Aunts, Uncles and Cousins as well. He wants to fly in to me then take a road trip down the coast which I have not done and I think it will be fun. He mentioned never being to Disneyland so I think we will be making it a stop. Sir only took us girls once, he was so stressed out that we stayed only half of a day. We were in middle school and looking back I realize all Sir saw was the bad people, all trapped in one place with his three little girls. I am surprised he did not have a stroke.

I booked Disneyland and text Eric that I took care of our road trip plans not wanting him to buy anything that will spoil my Christmas Present because I really do not know what to get him and I think Disneyland would be something we could both enjoy, together. My original idea was an engraved Gloc like the one he found in my bag but since this is my first boyfriend Christmas I do not want to mess it up.

When I get home I go nuts cleaning. Eric will be coming for Thanksgiving in a couple days and I have to make sure everything is perfect. Once everything is clean I do a walk though to make sure the dungeon is secure. I still need to go to Home Depot. Last summer I extended the back deck to run along the back of the house to the Master Bed room. I put in a French door in the Master to the deck and have no furniture for the back yard. I took out the old play set and added mulch in the yard to give it a HGTV home improvement look.

Since buying the house I have tried to make it my own. I eventually upgraded the appliances and redid the floors. Mom and Dad did some upgrades on the bathrooms and the garage over the years but most of their money went into the Maui condo. Living alone I had enough dishes and towels to get buy but Danielle had insisted we get nice new towels for display and guests and hid my every day one's in the closet. Danielle also took me to Anthropology to finally buy the comforter set I have been wanting. I do not normally buy things I do not need but Danielle gets me to treat myself every now and then. She is coming over with Matt's truck so I can go get my patio furniture.

While I sit in the back yard putting my new chairs and table together she starts going through my closet.

Danielle: "OMG I am purging half your closet. You have had these UGG boots since middle school. EWWWW"

Me rolling my eyes in a flat tone: " Thanks for your help."

Danielle: "Hurry up with that. When you are done we are going to Stanford. We will go shopping and get dinner. It is a must."

Me: "Yeah I will hurry"

I am regretting this already. I know I need new stuff and Danielle knows I dress good for work but I have a limited amount of regular clothing options. Plus I did want to go to Victoria's Secret anyway. Danielle is the only person I trust enough to steer me in the right direction when it comes to fashion. She is good and will be honest at the same time. I might as well do some Christmas shopping while we are there.

Danielle made us haircut and blow out appointments at Aveda so we hit it first. I hit the Giants store and get Eric a hat. I am looking forward to taking him to games. Danielle and I bought season tickets in college. We had this wild idea that if we were ever separated this would bring us together. She maxed out her credit card and I just paid cash, but acted like a broke college student cashing in her life savings. We have been seat buddies ever since. We even drafted a contract and everything. People think we are crazy but that is who we are. Matt even has to formally ask to borrow my seat and vice versa now that I have a boyfriend. There is nothing like a live Giants game.

I get a new purse at Kate Spade. I need a new black, simple bag. We both end up getting earrings too. I treat myself to two new pairs of jeans, new Vans; I get new leggings and sport bras, a new pair of UGGs and UGG slippers. Instead of Victoria's Secret Danielle insists on Rigby & Peller. It was a little more than I wanted to spend but I got some great things. I make Danielle hit up J Crew for some sweaters and we hit Niemen for a dress to wear for Thanksgiving. We finish up the trip with L'Occitane and La Baguette. Something about Stanford Shopping Center makes me happy. It is not just that I am a female that likes to spend money, it brings back memories of when my mom was still alive. We would always go school shopping, dance dress shopping and have a day eating and relaxing. The indoor/outdoor Polo store makes me miss her the most. She loved her polos.

I have a lot of laundry to do now but I put everything off until tomorrow and get ready for bed. Since Hawaii I put a TV in my bedroom. It feels weird but I like to zone out to whatever is on every now and then. Relaxing my phone starts to buzz.

Can't wait to see you. Kinda nervous

Me: *Why are you nervous?*

Just excited to see you I guess

Me: *Well Danielle and I went lingerie shopping today if that helps calm the nerves*

That doesn't help

Me: *Sorry*

It's been a while so I don't want to be awkward

Me: *When you get here lets just do it and get it out of the way*

So romantic

Me: *Just a suggestion*

I want it to be perfect

Me: *It will be fine*

You got me all worked up with your lingerie comment

Me: *Good*

You're killing me

Me: *I was going to take you to eat before bringing you home. May be we can just order in?*

Take me to dinner first. We can fuel up.

Me: *Oh God I don't want to know what your thinking*

You will find out soon enough

Me: *Miss you*
Miss you more
Me: *Good night*
Think of me

Thanksgiving

I do the girly, cute thing and wait for him to come out of the gate area with a sign with his name on it. He just smiles and hurries over. He picks me up and we kiss. People start looking at us smiling. He has his camouflage backpack so people more than likely think it's a long lost reunion. Nope, just started dating, nothing to see here. He looks great, blue jeans, vans, a black t-shirt and jacket, casual but so sexy.

I take him to Moss Beach Distillery. I have been craving it since the Danielle and Matt Great debate. Dinner is good and the view is amazing. Not only is Eric super hot but, we are seated by the window overlooking the ocean and I am loving every minuet. Eric fills me in on the guys and how Elle gave him a talk to about us. She wanted to make sure he was on his best behavior and used his manners when meeting my friends and no funny business unless he thinks we are serious. I had to laugh out loud. I cannot believe she grilled him like a mother. I am thankful she has my back.

Eric with a huge smile: "God, I love when you laugh like that."

Me: "I am glad you are hear."

Eric: "Me too."

The drive home hosted a lot of tension. When we pulled in the garage he said he would get his bags later, he needed a shower after his long flight. I did not think anything of it until he held my hand all the way back to my bathroom. It was like he had been to my house before, there we undressed and took a shower. The rest of the night was just Eric and I.

I have no idea what time we finally fell asleep but when I woke up he wasn't in bed. I got up, brushed my teeth and through on a t-shirt and his silkies. He was in the kitchen making breakfast for us. He set the table and was trying to figure out my ancient waffle maker when I snuck up behind him. In his distraction he ended up burning a waffle while we kissed in my kitchen. Not talking much, we ate then he took me back to my room for some more alone time. Things were easy with Eric. I liked not having to constantly make conversation. People were hard for me to navigate and Eric took control which made things less stressful for me.

My home phone rang and Eric got up to answer it. My home phone is in the kitchen mounted on the wall totally old school, but it is the one thing my mother picked out that I have left. It is pastel teal and tremendously ugly but I cannot get rid of it. I just hear Eric's laughter and wonder who he could be talking too: Danielle.

We meet Danielle and Matt at the Barn for burgers and beer. Danielle's eyes light up when she saw Eric walk in with his arm around my waist. Matt is intrigued too. We have known each other since grade school and Matt has never seen me with a guy. He probably thought I was a lesbian in hiding. Matt would never admit it but I think he is happy to be wrong, he is not one for uncomfortable situations.

Dinner is good. Eric likes my friends so far. Danielle dominated the conversation but Matt got some big brother type questions in. Eric was flawless in his answers and surprisingly really likes me. I guess I was good in bed after all and not completely awkward. We agree to meet Danielle at her moms around one tomorrow for Thanksgiving then head home.

Remembering it was Thanksgiving eve I had a little bit of a heavy heart remembering when my mom was still alive. As a family we would go into the city, eat Ghirardelli for dinner and since Christmas carols on the trolls around Union Square, just mom and us girls.

That night was much of the same as the previous night. No clothes and in bed. We did catch a movie, or at least parts of a movie. We talked a little and fell asleep. Thanksgiving day morning Eric did not make breakfast. I told him last night I would do shakes so we could save room for lunch and dinner. I took him for a run on the beach and even though it was so cold we actually attempted to go in the water. I think it was an excuse to head home, shower and warm up.

Thanksgiving with Danielle and Matt's families was fun. There were so many people we got bounced around. Eric teased me throughout the day on how many people commented on me actually having a boyfriend and they prayed and prayed it would happen someday. Thanks people. They all asked how we met, how long we have been together. Danielle's grandmother was the only one who asked if we were going to get married. Eric calmly responded "I have to get her to fall in love with me first." I think Danielle's grandmother is just pushy since I finally found a man interested in me.

We got home late and where both exhausted.

Eric: "Are holidays always like that with you?"

Me: "Only the ones when Danielle is involved."

Eric: "The wedding should be fun."

Me: "Tell me about it. It is going to be a Half Moon Bay event for sure."

Eric: "I am glad you invited me the weekend of the Shower. Matt was talking about getting a couple of the guys together for beers while you ladies have a blowout Bachelorette. Matt isn't interested in anything exciting. He just wants to chill."

Me: "You know what I have planned so you come over later in the night."

Eric: "Sounds like a plan."

The rest of the weekend we mostly just stayed in bed, catching up for lost time and being apart. We did make the drive down the coast to Santa Cruz making a couple beach stops on the way. He had never been to the bay so we hit some staples. Next time we will hit the city.

Before he left I drove him over the hill to see my high school and take him to eat at some old favorites of mine. We drove the Alameda to Millbrae then to the airport, he like the roadways, being different than when he grew up with. Before dropping him off we parked in a lot off the

El Camino to make out one last time. It was hard saying good-bye. I was a little surprised with myself when I tiered up when he buried his nose in the nape of my neck and whispered he was going to miss me so much. I really did not want this trip to end.

Flash Backs

With Eric gone I relay had no motivation to do anything once I got home. Sadly I started to think of my mom and our family holidays. This year will be the first time my sisters and I don't see each other at all. I know that as we grow we grow apart with our own lives. I understand it is part of the journey but my little flash back the other night got me thinking.

There was never a time when my mom and dad where not in sync. They always knew the others next move and always were in tune with what was going on around us and with each one of us girls. My mom always knew who every kid at school was and who lived in what neighborhood. She knew everyone in our neighborhood, even the odd man on the corner of Kehoe. It seemed he never came out of his home. We always teased each other he was a vampire because no one ever saw him out during the day and wondered what he ate. Stupid kid stuff really.

Every day life growing up was simple and easy. We had a schedule and for the most part everyone stuck to it. We were a busy family, always going from school to work or an after school activity. Our parents kept us involved and which kept us out of trouble. We always sat at the table for Sunday dinner as a family because the rest of the week was flooded with practice, work or some church volunteer function my mom always signed us up for.

I remember this one Halloween we decided to Trick-o-Treat in El Granada instead of our neighborhood. Mom and Dad were really bent out of shape about it. Mom had always stayed home and passed out candy and Dad took us from door to door. We were all around Middle School age and wanted to collect candy from the houses on Elm Street. The houses where significantly spaced out so we wouldn't really get very much but there was one house in particular that we all wanted to visit. It was an old home that had seen better days but the owners kept it up as best they could. They gave out king-size Snickers which was amazing. Every Halloween their house would be flooded with people because they would not decorate, but instead leave one lit Jack-o-lantern on their front porch. It was genius.

Dad took us to Elm Street with a laundry list of restrictions. We really only wanted to hit this one house and Dad was taking the fun out of it. That night was a little odd. I could have sworn I saw my mom between two of the houses we were at but everyone concluded I was just spooked out. After we hit up the Snickers house we heard sirens and Dad called it quits and took us back home. I will never forget how spooked out we were walking up to the front door of the Sinkers house. We were joined by three other kids and we were all scared out of our minds to ring the door bell. It was all good fun in the end.

Christmas Eve's at our house were the best. Mom and Dad always had people over, usually a couple families from the neighborhood, Danielle and her family, a couple of my sisters friends families and anyone who may want to come. None of our outside family could ever make it but that was all right. My mom would say it was a potluck party but end up making a bunch of food. Seven layer bean dip, hot wings, spinige dip, deviled eggs, fudge, shrimp cocktail, chips and salsa, guacamole, and us girls would make about one hundred decorated sugar cookies. It was a blast. No one exchanged gifts, it was just a time to spend with one another. We played board games and towards the end of the night everyone participated in a huge game of sharades. It is something I will remember forever. Everyone dressed up, laughing, talking and just being present with one another.

As good Catholics we were we always went either the Midnight Mass on Christmas Eve or the afternoon Christmas Day mass. Another huge holiday in our family was Easter. Mom and Dad would host our family for Easter every year. It would be a huge production the day before getting the food ready and Easter Sunday morning we would all get dressed in our Sunday best and meet at Mass as a family. Afterwards we would mingle with friends before heading home for lunch and according to my uncle David who wanted no part in any of it…Golf. The family gathered at our house where the younger kids would hunt for eggs in the back yard while the food cooked, the teenagers would gather in the family room to talk and the guy teenagers would go out front and play basketball in the driveway. My uncle David would walk in, sit on the couch and turn on Golf, did not talk to anyone and when it was time to leave would turn off the television, thank my parents and leave. He had to be higher than a kite because there were many times I fell fast asleep watching golf with him. The family mainly talked about food, ate a lot of my moms homemade bread and the adults drank a lot of wine. There was nothing special we did, just spent time with one another.

Growing up in Half Moon Bay we did not have the changing of the seasons or any seasons for that matter. We had sixty-five degree weather all year round, cloudy with the occasional sunny day. You always knew the fog would roll in at some point. Beach days were cold but it was something to do so we all made it work. The best was Fourth of July. Everyone hoped for a clear day though we all knew come dinner-time the clouds would roll in. We would still head down to the beach after dark to see the fireworks. Sometimes you could see them explode, other times make out the color behind the cloud cover and most years we were just able to listen to them. One year my parents had a great idea to go out on a boat with some friends of theirs. It was a fun day on the water but we saw nothing special once the fireworks started. It was just really cold at that point. Being out on the bay, in the middle of summer you still need pants and a jacket.

Thinking about the holidays I remember my first assignment I took during them. Mom was so pissed off at me and my Dad, I had to convince her it was a college internship and really important. I know she did not buy it one bit. So instead of being gone Thanksgiving through Christmas I was able to only miss Thanksgiving. Funny enough I was in Turkey. I think my dad orchestrated it that way to lighten the mood of my mom totally being pissed off I was gone.

I was to fly in as a American student studying abroad on Holiday. It was not a hard role to play. I was staying at a very low rate motel where there had been some backpackers. There was recent news that over the course of six months some backpacking groups would come through and loose a member before they left. Most people thought nothing of it, they may have met someone and taken off or gone back home. There are so many travelers that go through Europe these days kids hope from one group to the other all the time. Unless there is someone keeping tabs on them they are easy pickings. After some research Sir and I found out that these were not just random disappearances or kids going home. There was a person that would lure one person from the group away from time to time. The bodies were yet to be discovered but this man was a common denominator in all of the stories. My assignment was to go, confirm or deny the information we had and act accordingly.

By my second night in I had an idea who the man was I was just waiting for him to make his move. I was for sure he would see me as week and pick me as his next victim. I was surprised to observe I was not what he wanted. That night at the pub he started to talk with one of the guys in our group. I had made friends with this Columbia Student group. They were taking the semester off and touring the world. They were at the end of month one and had some fun stories. The man of interest picked up on one of the all American looking guys. He could have been on a poster at Hollister, blonde hair and blue eyes. He was physically fit and not a totally idiot either.

After the second round of beers came, the man reached to grab his beer from the center of the table where the waitress had left our pints and very smoothly dropped something into Hollister's beer. He had defiantly used that move before. After about twenty minuets the man suggested they go outside to try one of his new cigars and Hollister was all about it. Let me fill you in that the man looked to be around the same age as all of us college students. He was not the creepy old man that hurts women and children. He was a skilled physcopath and I could tell carefully planned out each person to ensure his needs were completely satisfied. He was not on a killing spree as some may label it. He took his time with each. I knew this by the time in between each disappearance, which made me realize he was a total sicko.

Five minuets after they left I got up to use the restroom. I was able to follow them undetected. The man had a loft apartment a couple blocks away from where we were all staying. After careful examination I realized no one else lived around this area. It was stores and shops that were all closed up for the night. He had chosen the perfect location as there was no foot traffic in this area after closing time. He was sections off on purpose. I was able to get inside without much effort. This was concerning because someone of his level should have more percasions in place. Standing in his kitchen I realized why he was relaxed about it. This is not the place were he takes his victims. Retreating I placed a couple cameras and returned to the bar.

The next day Hollister was out and about. I was able to listen in on the man all day long with my ear piece. He worked from home, made calls and ordered in lunch. After lunch is where I got my first clue. He called and invited Hollister for a drink at the old dive bar in the industrial district. Hollister agreed. That night I followed Hollister to the building where there was to be a secret underground local bar. Stupid Americans eat that shit up all the time and it gets them killed. Hollister was not even scared, walked right in, no questions. There was no lighting, no sounds, no sign of anyone. Idiot. As soon as Hollister passed the threshold the man captured him. I did a quick run down of the area, buildings and shipments over the last year going in and out of this block. I had maps, building layouts and pluming memorized. I choose to enter in a side door and that is when I came face to face with the weirdest works of art I had ever seen. The man had been a talented painter but the many works hanging throughout the open room, it was the content that made my stomach hurt. I think he killed, posed and painted these people. The smell was confirmation he kept the bodies for some time. The canvas he used where large so it must take months for him to finish a piece, which lines with the disappearances.

I was able to find Hollister drugged out laying on a couch, help the man with his drug overdose and alert the local police to suspicious activity happening in the area. The anonymous caller was taken seriously and a couple units were sent out to investigate. They found

Hollister, the paintings, the man dead and personal items from the past disappearances. They confirmed all the paintings were of missing persons and were able to contact the families of their findings. No bodies were ever recovered but the man took a chance with Hollister and lost. It looked as though he was planning to paint an Abercrombie type advertisement.

The Holidays

When Sir emailed me my next assignment I was thankful to have something to do for the next couple weeks. Eric would be flying in December 20th and staying through the New Year, but the time until then seemed to be passing slowly. I managed to get all my shopping done, watched a lot of TV and Danielle and I hit the city a couple days and then spent another day dress shopping. Presents were wrapped, packaged and sent.

Sir had me going to New York and Chicago for a couple of hits. Big City hits are easy and not uncommon. Sadly around the Holidays and leading up to the Super Bowl there is a lot of unwanted traffic in the States. I hope the people that live in ignorance of it all appreciate what happens behind the curtains to keep them safe.

New York is always fun. Holiday season shopping is in full swing and there are people everywhere. It is overall a nice place to visit but it is what happens in the dark corners and back corners of the clubs that brings me a paycheck. There is one club in particular only few know about. Very secretive, yet not so exclusive that when people going missing there is any thing for anyone to worry about.

New York and Chicago are seamless. No one actually died in public and I did not even have to get up close and personal. The bodies just started to fail two to four hours after their passing me. Depending on the dose I gave them, some did not even feel a thing. One was so drunk he passed out peeing in the alley of a not so good neighborhood should be interesting to hear the rumors, which stem from that.

After returning to San Francisco I stop at the office for my routine decompression and unloading. I leave my mustang and get a rental for Eric and I to drive down the coast. Since we will not be flying south but flying to Vegas for New Years I pack a small bag for security. I do not think we need a full bug out bag for our road trip, well at least no grenades.

Eric gets in late so we head straight home after I pick him up. We make some sandwiches before going to bed. Though we got to sleep later than expected we both wake up ready to go. Both excited for this adventure together. We stop at Half Moon Bay Bakery for donuts then hit the One.

We wander Santa Cruz for a couple hours before making it to Carmel. The next day we spend in Monterey and Carmel, eating good food and taking in the sights. In one of the stores I notice Eric eyeing a pair of Starfish earrings, so I ask, "Gold or Silver?"

Eric: "I think my mom would like them for Christmas."

Me: "Then get them for her. Is there any more shopping we need to be doing?"

Eric: "No, I got my dad gift card to Barns and Nobel so I am good."

Me: "Okay then get them for your mom."

The Bed and Breakfast we were staying at was so cute. White finishes and the ultimate beach house feel. Being it was cold we lit the fire at night and fell asleep watching the light dance. The next day we made our way down to San Louis Obispo. We made food stops on the way drawing the trip out. We made it to town around dinner, we just ordered in and made it a night to ourselves.

Christmas Eve we woke to Eric's mom calling us to see where we were. It was seven in the morning. We reported to his Aunts house a couple hours later. There was Christmas cookies being made and decorated, gift-wrapping and football on TV. His mom gave me the biggest hug. I guess though he dated his last girlfriend for a couple years he ever brought her home for the holidays. Mary, Eric's mother gave me a tour of the house and introduced me to the family. Eric and his dad Charles went outside to escape the chaos. Mary is such a sweet lady. Her mannerisms still reflect years as a Marine. Even Christmas cookie decorating was precise and planned.

After lunch we went back to our room to check out mentally for a while before having to report back to Grandmothers house for her Christmas Eve party. Eric's grandmother liked to have a formal affair. Not suit and Tie formal but close. Eric had warned me about it when he came for Thanksgiving so I made sure to get something while I was out shopping with Danielle.

After showers and some bedtime we did not want to get up and get ready. We were both so tired from earlier. Once we finally got up we both got ready fairly quickly. Eric wore navy slacks and matching jacket, a green button up shirt with brown dress shoes, no tie. I was speechless, he cleaned up nice, and I made sure to take a mental picture of him in this moment.

I caught Eric looking at me equally amazed. I opted for a burgundy velvet dress, fitted, high collard with three quartered sleeves. Being a little cold outside I wore black tights with black strappy shoes. I wore my hair down with a simple curl. I think he really like what he saw. He moved close and buried his nose in the nape of my neck and hair. My heels were extra high, for the first time I was almost as tall as him.

We didn't speak to each other on the drive to his grandmothers house, upon entering we were bombarded with pictures. I think we must have posed for over one hundred pictures. His mom had to take at least fifty. We took pictures next to the tree, next to the fireplace, out on the porch, with his parents, with his grandparents, mostly just him and I. When it was finally over his dad brought us each a scotch.

Dinner was wonderful and so was desert. We ate so much food we could barley move from our seats. Once dinner was over the family moved into the large living room to exchange gifts. His extended family opened presents on Christmas Eve; Christmas day was designated solely for immediate family. I got a few gifts from his family. It was a lot to take in but an experience I will never forget. After everyone was done opening gifts the family started to play charades. I took a second to text Danielle. We always send each other something on Christmas Eve and Christmas Day, BFF Traditions. When I look at my phone I see I have fifty-seven messages. I scroll through and I have one from Boomer, Elle and Danielle, the rest are pictures from Mary. I take a minuet to save them all.

Eric is waiting for my return with a puzzled look on his face. I explain the influx of pictures I had to sift through and he just laughs. He wants to see them later tonight. We hang out for another hour then make our way back to our room. Entering the room I notice something is different. I become alert and start to survey my surroundings. Relaxing I see there are rose petals and candle-lights leading to the bedroom.

He takes my hand and leads me to the bed. There is champagne and deserts waiting for us.

Eric: "Merry Christmas."

Me: "Merry Christmas."

Eric: "You look amazing in that dress but…."

"Wow, I wasn't expecting that."

Point for me, I made sure he did not see me get dressed earlier so I could wear something special for him tonight. I am glad he likes it, I think he loves it. I help him out of his suit when he blurts out: "I love you." With that we dive into the best Christmas Eve a girl could ever ask for.

Christmas morning in a hotel will never been my favorite but with Eric I don't mind. I slide out of bed to get his gift. When I return to the room he is sitting up in bed with a package on his lap. I wonder where is came from. I have him open my gift first. I got him the ultimate Disneyland Package. He laughs so loud I know he is excited about it. It will be a blast. He hands me my gift, a small teal box and I hold it for a while.

Eric: "Open it already"

I unwrap the white bow to find a small, delicate necklace. He picked out a sweet gold necklace with a diamond pendent. Speechless I just stare at it. No one has ever given me such a beautiful gift before. I have a feeling he put a lot of thought into it

Eric concerned: "Do you like it?

Me: "Its beautiful. I love it."

Eric: "More than you love me?"

Me: "Not even close."

Eric: "I had trouble picking it out for you. I could not decide then Boomer mentioned it looked like the end of a bullet so I figured it was the perfect gift."

Laughing: "Anything you picked would have been perfect."

Eric: "Even socks?"

Me: "Anything."

The rest of the morning was ours. We didn't leave the bed until it was time to meet his parents for Christmas Day Dinner at his aunts. We dressed nice but casual. Eric wore black jeans; a black t-shirt and a black leather jacket, which made him, look even sexier than normal. I opted for black skinny jeans, a black top and a fluffy sweater. One would think we coordinated but I guess we were just falling into sync with each other.

The next morning we took our time getting packed and made our way down to Los Angelas. We hit up the Hollywood sign and made our way to Disneyland. We are staying at the Disney Grand Californian and I cannot wait for Eric to see it. I have hear it is the best Hotel to stay at and wanted to go all out, it is a present that keeps on giving. I am not sure how Eric is going to react but we drop off our bags and head to the Spa. I booked us a coffee body polish and I know I am really going to love it.

The resort is plush. The cabin feel and the attention to detail has us both spinning. Eric did not mind the treatment but would have rather spent the time alone in our bedroom. We ordered room service and called it a night before our day of riding every ride tomorrow. When we get up I lay out our matching t-shirts to see if he says anything. I put mine on and notice he hesitates before putting his on too. In his jeans, t-shirt and Giants hat, I am in love. I want to be comfortable for the long day ahead of us so I am dressed the same. We are totally matching and scream new couple! The weather is cold so I grab my olive bomber jacket and he grabs a flannel and we take off. We get early entry into California Adventure and he asks me to put his wallet in my purse. I guess that's what couples do.

With no plan, we make our way left and hit every ride on our way. As we loop around to Hollywood land we get in line to take pictures with every character we find. We have no plan but to do as much as possible. Bugs life is lame but we ride every ride anyway. Cars land has to be our favorite. We ride everything a couple times before hitting Ghirardelli Square up for lunch. We grab some drinks and continue our quest through California Adventure. Since the Disneyland Parade starts before the water show we head over to Disneyland. The cold weather does not stop us from riding everything we can. As we make our way over to the Haunted Mansion we get begets and hot chocolate. It is all so much fun.

Eric: "Is this what it is going to be like being with you?"

Me: "If fun and adventure is what you mean.... then yes."

Eric: "Do you ever think we wont have a good time together?"

Me: "We enjoy doing nothing so I think we are good."

Eric: "I do not want this to end."

Me: "Wait until tomorrow night and you may be over this place completely."

Eric: "That's not what I meant and you know it."

Me: "I am just as serious as you about US even though my present wasn't as romantic."

Eric: "This is the most romantic week of my life, and I have you to thank for it."

Me all shy: "Oh, stop."

Eric: "I love you."

Me: "I love you too."

Disneyland was a world win. When it was time to leave Eric still did not know what our next stop was. We had to stop at the post office to mail home some of our Christmas Gifts. We droped off the rental car and check into our flight to Vegas. Eric had no idea and is asking me every question imaginable. I tell him nothing. When Danielle asked me what I was planning, she signed her and Matt up to meet us there. Neither one of us has ever done New Years Eve outside the city before, at least not celebration wise. I did spend a couple New Years Eve's working. It is actually the easiest night of the year to take out targets. It was almost a competition with Sir one year to see how much damage we could do. I won.

We catch a cab to The Bellagio and get checked in. Our room over looks the fountains and I am excited to eat. Vegas, for how dirty and shady it can be does have some of the best restaurants and live shows. We eat and hit one of my favorite shows then call it a night. We are tired from Disneyland so we snuggle up and relax.

Eric: "I am not going to like being away from you."

Me: "We will figure it out."

Eric: "I am set to be gone for long periods of time soon."

Me: "I will cry every night until you come home."

Eric very serious: "Its not funny. Being with me comes with its hardships."

Me: "Yes, your looks are hard to get past but I did say I love you."

Eric: "Be serious for a second. I really want us to work. This has all been amazing but reality is around the corner."

Me: "I have been alone my whole life. I can be alone and I am ok waiting for you. I don't want to lose you and have no intentions of changing my mind. I am set in my ways now, which include you."

Eric: "Good. You know the guys are going to ask if we got married in Vegas. It is kind of what Marines do. Rush weddings."

Me: "Lets have a real wedding then. Elvis is cool and all but I kind of would like the real thing. Helping Danielle with hers has been inspiring."

Eric: "Deal"

The glitter and glam of a Vegas New Years Eve party mixed with all the kissing and future talk had my head spinning. It was almost like a dream. Flying home with out Eric gave me a moment to recalibrate. He had to fly to San Diego to meet up with some other Marines before heading back to the islands. Getting home I took my time to unpack. Printed all of our pictures and started a picture book. It may be lame but since Eric is my first boyfriend I am going to girl out for this.

What I Do

On my flights across the world for my next assignment I daydream of my road trip with Eric. I laugh out load thinking of The Little Mermaid ride, we had to ride it twice because the first time we rode it we missed the entire ride because we were too busy making-out.

I can't help but wonder what it would be like to be in a domestic relationship with him. I really do not see us in those roles. I guess it is why we work. The couple days before I left it was constant text wars with Eric. Him getting ready for his trip, his team along with the twenty other guys were getting split up into smaller teams and sent to different locations to gather information on the common denominator of their missions. Boomer and him got assigned Mexico City with a guy named Travis. They leave the day after tomorrow. I told him I was flying to London for work. Technically I am flying to London, just not staying.

For the next two weeks I am going on a bender and trying to get as much work done as possible. I have to get back to London for my Marketing Conference. I do plan to meet with some clients. If my work is not done I will just stay longer and site see. I really have nowhere to be since Eric will be back in Hawaii by then.

I start in Lithuania and make my way to Croatia, the Vatican City then back to London. In all reality I could have made my stay in London action packed. There has been an influx of crime and trafficking in London. I am out of ammo and supplies so I stop at my dad's safe house to reload. There I can check in with my dad and see if anything new is on the radar and or calendar. My Marketing Conference goes about a week but I can get some extra work done at night. My dad says there is a gentleman staying in my hotel that will be receiving a shipment later this week that I can handle. Apparently he is just a customer but a customer that disposes of his merchandise when he is finished. He never keeps anything longer than a week and only likes virgins.

I get what I need and head back to my room. My Conference is huge. Every major Firm is represented, all trying to land the biggest clients. I would be happy with one decent client from the list presented this week. One foreign client would allow me to sped a little more without raising any red flags on my taxes. I still try to maintain a upper middle class image and my bookkeeping is perfect. My company is small but I do very good work. I help my clients. I actually can take the time each one needs because it is just me. And I can add my other work in to fill up the time. I am not one of the field agents that pads the books with my other income.

The second day is filled with guest speakers. I am not entirely excited about this portion but it looks good to clients when you take the time to emerge yourself in what is new and upcoming, it is all for face value. I spot my target. He is wealthy and is very well guarded. His guards are dressed just as lavish as he is, all of them with Rolex's and Armani suits. I know he will not always be guarded. It is known that no one is allowed in his room when he is there, except for his purchases. Guards are present when the room is cleaned or when there is a delivery, otherwise the room is fully secure.

When we break for lunch I am able to slip in and get a lay of the land. No cameras or bugs, these guys did most of my work for me already, I know there would be no trail left, these types do not want any evidence. It has even been know that his guards have stolen the sheets and burned them so there is no DNA evidence. If you do not want anyone to know what you are doing, you may not want to be doing it then. He pays his staff well to keep quiet and everyone knows if you talk you die. Loyalty is life, what a market. I make a mental note and head back. I am in and out without a trace.

More lectures and meetings make the time to pass so slowly. I have been checking my phone periodically to see what Eric is up too. Tonight I will make my move on old Mr. Subplantat. When I get into his room the young girl is tied up in the corner, fuck when did she arrive? She was not supposed to arrive until tomorrow; I guess he could not wait. I check her pulse and she is still alive thank god. I need to tell Sir. Something about this does not feel right. I make my way to the bathroom and take him out in his bubble bath. As I make my way back through the room the girl calls to me for help. She's from Lithuania so I respond back in Lithuanian, which makes her cry.

Girl: "Please help me. Please kill me."

Me: "I can't. He is dead, he can't hurt you anymore."

Girl: "But someone else will. They will always find someone else until I am too old. Please kill me now. I can not live like this anymore."

Me: "I have never killed an innocent before."

Girl: "You will be saving me from pain beyond your scariest dreams. Please save me from this Hell. I will never have a normal life after what he has done to me tonight."

I responded with a node and a prick to her forearm. She closed her eyes with a smile knowing she would finally be in peace. I went back to my room and did not leave for twenty-four hours. I have never cried so hard in my life. I thought killing the evil I was helping but I am only putting a dent in a much larger picture. There are no survivors; there was no happy ending for those girls and boys and the others in her circle. What about them? What about the victims?

Eric calls and I break down to him, I just cry. I bet he thinks I am on my period or something like that. Listening to him talk about his findings help calm me. I miss him so much. Life with him is so much easier than all this darkness I deal with. Why is there so much evil? I picture the girl's eyes, volumes of thanks as I agreed to help her. She was truly happy for once, and I am sad of how it had to happen.

I checked in on the hotel to see if there was any buzz about the sexual predator and his child sex slave but no word up front. On the back end the guards found both of their bodies the following morning when they went inside the room ten minuets after he was suppose to come out. The guards handled everything so the hotel had no clue about two murders on property. I was able to ping the number they called to report the incident. They had new orders and a new person to work for, they were checking out of the hotel as I made my way down to the restaurant for dinner.

I over hear the men talking in Croatian about the Marines in search of the Tsar, the one who makes the rules and head of some gang right now. I guess that is who Sir is looking for. I am exhausted with myself and my embarrassing emotional break down to Eric so I ask for my food to be delivered to my room. The concierge stops me as I pass the desk and offers me a package that arrived for me. The guards look at me a mumble 'pathetic girl' in Russian. They are stunned when I make eye contact and take off. If they only knew how pathetic I really am.

Something inside of me changes and I promise myself I will hunt them down too. If you do not stand up for what is right you are apart of the problem. Those men are by no means innocent, they knew what was going on and turned a blind eye. In some versus that makes you even worse. No amount of money is worth that life.

The package is a satellite phone sent by my dad. He knows what happened and I break down to him too. I tell him everything and he is okay with my decision to help her. In this work we cannot help everyone by just taking out the evil of the world. Sometimes we have to set souls free. He told me a story of his mentor, an older woman that died ten years ago. She sent my dad to Egypt to break up a child camp; the camp was so large it was using an old orphanage building as a front. Children would come in and out but never allowed to speak to anyone. When my dad arrived he made his way and searched every level and every room. It was filthy, the only showers where in the basement where the clean special rooms where. They would only clean the kids before they sent them into the rooms for services. Men would come in the back entry so no one would suspect otherwise. My father was so horrified by the look in the children's eyes he lost himself for a moment. They all looked like hollow shells of what were suppose to be people, some with wounds and scares from torture. Sexual pleasures were not the only thing being sold there. Back then Sir was COMM'd into his handler and she gave him an order to blow the place. He was stunned and could not move until she yelled at him over the COM to light the place up. He followed orders then took the next week off. After meeting up with her to go over the mission she did not even allow him to speak. She dove into her explanation: "All lives in that building were lost. What those children had been exposed to, Death was an escape, and Living would have been constant torture. Not only were there five targets in the building but also a meeting being help upstairs with seven men about a larger shipment needed to replace the used up ones. It was the only call to make. Next time you wont need me to make it for you."

The truth hurts sometimes but she was right. I did the right thing but it still did not sit right with me. Sir explained that it was after that he realized the meaning behind of their work. No one should ever have to endure that pain or experience that kind of violation. The world has its issues but just to save one life from that is all he can work towards.

I know I have to keep going to save at least one child. I know I have to keep going to protect the ones I love and the generations to come. I can do this. I will do this and now I will be better than ever.

Babe you doing ok?

Me: *Yeah better, sorry for the breakdown*

That's what I signed up for. The good the bad and the ugly

Me: *Thanks*

Really, are you better?

Me: *Yeah. Just dove into work full bore and it caught up to me. All the travel with no sleep kicked me in the butt.*

I know that feeling

Me: *You cry too?*

LOL no but if you need me too Ill try

Me: *No you're fine*

I know that's why you love me

Me: *That's not the only reason*

I might be able to swing up your way before heading back to the island

Me: *Really? When?*

Two days?

Me: *I'll be home*

You sure?

Me: *Yeah, I am over London*

Will you take me next time?

Me: *Sure but can we wait a while?*

Yeah. I want to travel the world with you

Me: *Can we just spend some time in bed first?*

Sounds great to me

Eric came in late and left thirty-six hours later. It was much needed R & R. We didn't leave my room. We ordered Round Table Pizza and Indian Take out. We talked about the dead ends he found in Mexico and the good food he ate. Boomer was in heaven with the ladies and their friend had to gain about ten pounds eating at this one taco truck they hit every day. I did not have to talk too much about my trip being it was lectures and meetings, nothing worth sharing.

Before Eric left he pulled out a little teal box from his bag.

Eric: "Sorry I did not have much time to get you something more meaningful, but Happy Birthday."

Me: "How did you know?"

Eric: "I snuck a peek at your id when we flew for New Years."

Me: "Thank you so much."

Eric: " Well, open it."

Me: "I love them. They match the necklace you got me for Christmas. Love you."

Eric: " I notice you do not wear any jewelry often and when I asked Danielle about it she told me you don't buy it for yourself. So I wanted to get you something that was special."

Danielle

The next couple weeks flew by. I was in full Maid of Honor mode getting everything finalized for Danielle's bachelorette. Eric was the only one who knew what I planned and I was so excited about it. I thought about telling Matt a couple things but I knew there was no way he could keep it a secret from Danielle. We will all be staying at the Ritz Half Moon Bay, where we will have dinner at the Conservatory then make our way to the patio where we will have our own personal concert set up. Drinks to follow, that way no one has to drive and we can dance all night. It is not the strippers most would plan but my party is going to be perfect. Per the invitations there is a dress code, which will set Danielle apart. We will have wristbands so the staff will know who is apart of our party for the games and drinks. I'm taking care of the tab but minimizing it to 2 drinks per wristband, after that they are on there own. I know this group so I am really protecting my pocketbook here.

Danielle calls me a couple times trying to question me about what to wear and where to go. Transportation has been taken care of and Matt has the dress she will be wearing the night of. He has specific instructions and is happy to play apart in this. Danielle always holds the cards and he is feeling mighty having something she can't have yet.

Valentines Day rolls around and since Eric and I won't be seeing each other for another week I send him a gift. He video chats me when he gets home to tell me all about the embarrassing moment he had opening his gift in front of all the guys. I originally sent it to Elle to pass along because I do not know the guys exact schedule. I know I could just look it up but it is nice to have another female friend in my life.

Since Elle had the baby before Christmas, her and I have been communicating more and more. I check in and she sends me pictures. She asks a lot about Eric, she talks to me like Eric's big sister. I find it comforting to know he has so many people who love him, it is a true sign of the kind of man he is and I am happy in my decision to love him. She has sent me a coupe of pictures of Eric holding the baby. It really makes me wonder if that could be us. He looks like a natural but I am not so sure I could be like her. She is flawless, so loving and understanding. Up until I met Eric I thought I was void of most emotions.

Apparently Elle gave it to the Kid to bring to Eric today. The Kid forgot all about it until they had an afternoon break and upon seeing it the guys made him open it up right then and there. I am glad I did not send anything kinky. I got him a Benchmade D2 Steel blade knife with 'I love you more' engraved into it. The guys gave him so much shit the rest of the day. He was impressed how thoughtful it was and accepted my challenge. We have been saying I love you more lately and I guess we are going into competition mode. He told me he was hand delivering my gift when he came, which got me giddy.

He came in the Wednesday before the shower and party. I picked him up at the airport but instead of going home we had to make a pit stop first. We stopped at Victoria's Secret to pick up my gift baskets. Eric was reluctant to enter at first but I made him a deal what ever he picked out I would wear, this kept him busy while I picked out twenty seven pairs of panties and matching bras. I had the lady up front wrap them all up in individual sets each with a gift receipt. Eric had picked me out something I would not have guessed but I assume he may have taken my offer as a challenge, game on Eric. When we got back to my house we unloaded and he asked if we could please eat. Sadly Half Moon Bay does not offer more delivery options so we jumped in the car and drove to San Benito House.

By the time we made it home we were both so tired we showered and crashed out. I woke first in the morning and put on my Victoria's Secret purchase. Eric was not expecting to wake up to me in it which lead to a lot of "I miss you's." Finally he gave me my Valentines Day gift which was a beautiful Hawaiian woven basket with Kona Coffee, macadamia nuts, Hawaiian barbecue chips, Hawaiian barbeque sauce, Hawaiian shortbread cookies, Plumeria soap, lotion and a Hawaiian print towel. It was everything I said I liked when we first met. He took the time to hunt it all down and put it together. He started to kiss me when he noticed my eyes got glossy. It was a good gift, the most thoughtful ever.

We spent the rest of the day hanging out he helped me trim my big tree in my backyard. After that was time to eat. I have noticed that Half Moon Bay has decent food now that Eric comes to visit me. We are always eating out. We end up at Safeway so we can get some food for the house. He wants to make me his mother's lasagna since I take him out all the time. I do not object and we pick out some wine on the way out. Tomorrow is going to be a long afternoon so I am thankful for staying in. He makes dinner and we actually eat at my dinner table.

Eric: "Would you ever consider moving away from here?"

Me: "Yeah, I used to live in the city."

Eric: "No I mean away from the Bay Area."

Me confused: "Yeah, I don't have any objections. Why you ask?"

Eric: "I just don't think I would ever get stationed anywhere near here."

Me: "I didn't think of that. Are they going to be moving you?"

Eric: "No but I been thinking about how to be closer to you."

Me: "We will figure it out."

Angela's shower was beautiful. Her parents have a ranch outside of town. There is a huge house on the hill and two football fields of grass that are separated by a creek. It is a picturesque property, we always loved coming over to just run wild when we were kids. It is set back in the mountain and is surrounded by trees as if you are not smack dab in the middle of the Bay Area. Angela has arranged the tables to be set up on the grass with patio string lights draped overhead. She as a small stage/ dance floor combo near the back porch with a sound system set up to play music for the guests.

Danielle and Matt enter and are introduced to the party. Champagne is being served so Eric and I take a glass. We have assigned seat so we go to find out table. Each table is decorated with sunflowers and a picture of Danielle and Matt.

Eric: "Please tell me when we get married we do things a little more low key."

Me: "Deal"

Everything is beautiful and detailed. The present table is over flowing and people are having a wonderful time. When Angela announces it is time for dinner, everyone makes their way to their assigned seat where they are served wine as salads start to arrive.

Me: "My sister had hers at the Distillery, remember that place? It was so good and low key."

Eric: "Logan and Elle had there's in their back yard. It was perfect."

Me: " I bet. They have a great property. I bet it was hard to find."

Eric: "When you come next we should check some houses out for fun."

Me: "That would be fun."

Dinner was great, desert was wonderful and even the light dancing was special afterwards. It was a warm party though very over the top. There where so many gifts I am not sure if Danielle and Matt have anything left on their registry. The best part of the night was introducing everyone to Eric, people that I have known my whole life where amazed I had such a good-looking boyfriend. It was a blow to the ego, I think I am good looking enough; I know they just were referencing how easily I am forgotten. We did get asked when we were getting married a couple times, apparently my biological clock is ticking how old did people think I was?

When we finally left Eric thanked me for inviting him.

Me: "Of course why wouldn't I have?"

Eric: "You invited me when we were first started dating remember?"

Me: "True, but I knew I liked you then."

Eric: "You did? I couldn't tell."

Me: "I had to keep it cool."

Eric: "I liked you from the moment I saw you."

Me: "When Boomer asked me to the table at Ululani's?"

Eric: "No, when you walked up from the beach. I will always remember that day."

Me: "I am glad I got to experience that with you. I know how important she is to you guys."

Eric: "I love you"

Me: "I love you more."

The drive home was mostly quiet. It was nice just being in each other's company. Eric broke the silence when he asked: "I didn't mean to be so forward about wanting our wedding a certain way. I know we just started dating."

Me: "It was forward but I agree"

Eric: "So you have thought about it?"

Me: "Yes I actually have."

Eric: "You're the first person I have been with that I have thought about it with."

Me: "We do get along quite well."

Eric: "We sure do."

The next morning I put Eric to work helping me get everything set up for the big night. I barked orders at him and he responded with a big smile and yes mama. I got us a room at the Ritz, knowing Eric would be joining us later. We took the opportunity to shower and relax before reporting for Maid of Honor duty.

Eric: "I liked it when you were barking orders at me earlier. So out of character for you and I like it."

Me: "What, I am authoritative."

Eric: "Not like that, it was sexy."

For some reason Eric brings a whole new element to my life. I am the pretty girl, the sexy girl, and the princess everyone dreams about. With him I am alive, relaxed and can break out of my normal ridged, planned out life. I do not have to be ten steps ahead of him and I am, in fact mostly five steps behind. He always has a jump on me. I am taken a back and blindsided with his affection towards me, I really was blown away with his marriage comment last night and still can not get over he said it and actually means it.

Eric was watching some sport on TV when I walked out of the bathroom, being that it is always cold in Half Moon Bay I opted for a black lace tank top with black high wasted skinny jeans, a black Gucci belt and some black ankle boots. My hair was loose and wavy and I wore my signature Eric gifts along with a layered gold necklace. His face when he saw me was golden; I did a little happy dance inside. He was off the bed in one swift movement and had me in his arms.

Eric: "I do not think you are going to make your party babe."

Me: "Sorry but I gotta run."

Eric: "I think you dress like that on purpose to get me going."

Me: "You know me too well."

Eric: "Please just stay with me."

Me: "I would love to but I have to be downstairs to welcome my guests."

Eric: "Will you wear that again for me?"

Me: "You bet."

Eric: "Will you wear my silkies again too?"

Me (slightly puzzled on the fascination of the Silkies): "Sure."

And with that I kissed him goodbye and headed downstairs for dinner. Everything was set up just how I envisioned it, sleek and sexy. Upon entry the girls received their Victoria's Secret gift basket with their party wristband inside. It has a switch that lights up, for the concert I wanted something fun for us along with the staff knowing who belonged to our group.

Dinner was great we made our way to the patio for the grand finale. Danielle was so surprised she started screaming like a mad woman. The small stage was set up and our High School no named favorite band was on stage ready to perform for us. Eric and Matt snuck in behind us about three songs into the concert. Matt was going wild and jumped right in front stage. Eric hung back with me and we swayed to the music.

Eric: "God I love you."

Me: "Love you too handsome."

We snuck off before the end of the show to be alone at last. We had a full weekend together but I really couldn't wait for it to be just us. We checked out the next day in a daze, I think the thought of us being apart was starting to hit both of us.

OMG Check your FB

Not knowing what Danielle was so excited about I scanned through my feed. I really only have a Facebook for work to allow people to know I am human. Eric's profile picture was of the two of us last night. He had asked a waiter to take a picture of us when he brought down my sweater. Looking at it I almost did not recognize myself.

Me: "So its official then."

Eric with a big goofy smile: "Well if Facebook says so then it must be real."

Me: "It's a good picture of us. Will you send it to me?"

Eric: "Already did."

Me: "Thanks, I never check my phone when I am with you."

Eric: "Why would you need to, you got all you need right here."

Me: "I'm sad you have to leave."

Eric: "Come with me."

Me: "I really want to."

Eric: "We will figure it out. When I get back from my next MAGTF I will come straight here as soon as I can."

Here we go again

The guy's last mission was considered a M.E.B. Marine Expeditionary Brigade, which means they had a specific task. I think it was for them to all die but that thankfully that did not happen. Now they will be going on a M.A.G.T.F., which is an Marine Air-Ground Task Force and Eric is expected to be gone right up until Danielle's wedding.

I am not looking forward to him being gone. Having him in my life has broken up the mundane of my killing sprees. One option Sir gave me was to follow them and protect them. As good as that sounds I think it is a waste of resources. I can just dive into work to distract me from the fact Eric and I are going to be apart for so long.

Elle sends me a picture of the guy's as they are ready to take off. She keeps me in the loop. I think it is comforting for her to know she has a friend that is going through the same emotions as she is seeing her man off.

I know the men will be in Romania and then part of the Sudan. I think their mission is half research for Richard and the other half government mandated routine follow-ups. Eric did not give me specifics and I have not yet looked into their files to find out. I have been self loathing since Eric left. Everything is clean and orderly but I have not done much of anything else. I have become a TV watcher and have gotten sucked into a couple shows. I fully understand now how Danielle wasted a whole weekend binge watching The Saprano's.

When I finally get bored and cant watch TV any longer I head to the office, clean and get things ready for my next assignment. Sir sent me my marks a couple days ago but I have yet to get on it. Once I map everything for the next month I get a work out in before heading home. I eat a peanut butter and jelly sandwich for dinner at my kitchen table and reminisce when Eric and I had the same meal for dinner not that long ago.

We didn't even want to get out of bed, before him I would have never thought I would ever have a lazy day. I do not think I have ever had one before him either. We were hungry but did not want to make an effort for anything and thankfully I had all the right ingredients. We just ate and laughed like we were in grade school again. Being with Eric is easy. He confided in me that since we have been together his nightmares are less and less. He still struggles with that one mission. It went south fast and the damage it caused was great. I know the story but I will let him tell me when he is ready.

Sir left me some information on that mission I found confusing. I have read the report over and over and I feel like there is a major component missing. I know the answer is staring us all in the face but we cannot pin point it. If only we could all have a pow-wow to discuss it, sadly that cannot happen. Who is going to believe a Marketing specialist can get her hands on classified Intel? No one.

In preparation for my next trip I secure my house. Just in case someone decides they want to break in, they will never know about or have access to the dungeon. It is a process but Sir had it as a security measure when he originally bought the house. Technology back then was far more advanced than any one was lead on too. He told me later on that it was in case we girls got mischievous while he was away at work. With that said I am surprised we never found anything because we would get into all sorts of messes.

I have an alert on my laptop in case Eric tries to video chat me. While I am away I really do not have access to anything to video him on. I am constantly changing numbers and phones. There is no way I can schedule a time to see him. This is one part of the relationship and job I am going to have to figure out. I guess I could just do week-by-week calls and return to my designated location each time, I just have been so spoiled doing what I want when I want I feel the extra effort is a pain in the ass. I really should have thought this through.

I originally thought going hard with work while Eric was gone was the way to go but with him as a new layer in my life I have to start planning better. As I am self loathing on my foolishness I get a ping he is trying to video chat me. It is not Eric but Elle. She called to let me know the guys are not going to be able to talk to us for a couple more days. Logan was able to get her a message and she promised Eric she would pass the information along. We chatted a bit before the baby started to cry then she was gone.

My self-loathing turned into sadness being that I cannot talk to or see Eric. I was hoping to see him one last time before I left. My house is more of a home when he is here. His comment about living closer to each other comes to mind. I wouldn't mind living together. Too bad he could not move here. I know he loves Hawaii and once people get stationed there they tend not to want to leave. If and when we ever did live together I would have to have the house remolded while he was away. I do not know if I would ever get so lucky. I might have to get my dad involved with that.

Waking up the next morning in reality I get my stuff and I head out. Day dreaming about the possible future is fun though, but now I have to focus. Crime rates in Europe have increased with the flux of refugees and other travelers. This makes my job easier though being in these places with all the low lives puts a damper on what were the worlds most loved destinations.

I will be staying in London and be branching out from there. Per my marketing itinerary I will actually be meeting two clients here in London, one in Spain, two in Italy, and one in Holland, all companies hoping to hit the major American City markets. This divides my time well with the locations and people I have to take care of.

My second body in, 'Dream on' by Aerosmith was playing on his radio and it has been playing over and over in my head since. It is like a symphony of Steven Tyler every time I meet someone and every time I killed someone. If I knew how to dance I could ballet into my targets home and leap over, taken him out and twirl away as *Dream on* sounds off in my head. I think I need to stop taking on such long assignments, even though I did this to myself I feel like I am starting to relate to the lyrics:

> *Live and learn from fools and*
> *From sages*
> *You know it's true, oh*
> *All these feelings come back to you*
> *Sing with me, sing for the years*
> *Sing for the laughter, sing for the tears*
> *Sing with me, just for today*
> *Maybe tomorrow, the good Lord will take you*
> *away*

I am thankful to finally hear from Eric. I need the distraction. They have been making slow progress but have a couple leads. He gets sappy at the end saying how much he misses me and that he is thankful to have me in his life. Man my life has changed so much. I am happy to have a relationship, though it is by no means normal.

I have been keeping track of Eric and the boys to ensure their safety. Finishing up in Holland I feel a load off my shoulders. As I head back to the States I travel through Canada to check on some information Richard received a few nights ago. I had some time to kill in Holland as I finished up earlier than expected. I started to look through the guy's files on what they had so far, what and who they were looking for and ideas on which they thought might be after them. Richard wrote off this one guys as a false lead without an interrogation. Fortunately I have the time and resources to help out.

Niagara Falls Canada is a great place to visit, and when you are over Canada you can just walk across the border to New York. Not having seen the sights myself I make it a perfect cover to make this detour on my way home. As I am walking around taking pictures and being the best sightseer I can I notice a commotion down the street. Thinking it is a street performer I walk over, only to find a man laying on his side. My natural instincts go into high gear. I walk around, surveying the people in the crowd and then see the face of the man. It is who I was looking for. I make sure I look horrified enough then bolt out of there.

The nice thing about New York there is still pay phones and enough shady back corners to get a burner phone without raising suspicion. I call Sir immediately and fill him in on everything, everyone I saw and every detail of the crime and Richards findings. Sir ordered me to get home and hung up. I wiped down the phone of any trace of myself and handed to a homeless man who thanked me before trying to sell it for booze.

I called Eric just in time; I have been so good on making our scheduled calls I do not want to screw up now.

Eric: "Miss you babe."

Me: "Same. I never thought it would be so hard to be away from you. I wonder how Elle does it."

Eric: "This kids are a good distraction I think. May be I can help you out with that for next time."

Me: "Funny. I am not ready to give up this body for a baby yet. Plus I am not married."

Eric: "I do like that body."

Me: "I know your coming for Danielle's wedding but may be we can take a trip together after. We will have to sync calendars."

Eric: "Where should we go? Somewhere warm so I can look at you in a bikini the whole time."

Me: "Oh god you are going to be an animal when you get home."

Eric: "Your animal now. Sorry."

Me: "I can deal."

Eric: "So may be Tahiti?"

Me: "That would be nice. A hut over the water."

Eric: "Okay, so you plan it and Ill get you my schedule once I know."

Me: "Deal."

Once back home I started planning our trip. I know exactly what and where we are going to go. I am so excited. But sadly I do not know when it will happen. What if we never get a chance to go? What if when he gets back he is not interested in me anymore? There are so many variables. I know people make it like Elle and Logan but I am afraid. I really love him.

No wonder I have never been in a relationship before. Planning a murder is easier. Danielle and I meet at Meza Luna and she goes over her plans for the Honeymoon. She has been planning it for a while and finally everything is final. They will be flying over to Switzerland and then Iceland. She has their two weeks booked with sight seeing and experiences. I hope my honeymoon is somewhere relaxing.

I am taking a trip to Russia to take on a few more assignments and attempt to track down the man behind the false Marine Mission. Sir has been dedicated to his fellow brothers and helping Richard (anonymously) and has two leads. He will be tracking the other one in China. I am excited to get back to business. With Eric being gone I feel it is much harder to keep myself distracted these days.

I spent one whole day after my dress fitting, trying on wedding dresses. Eric has made a couple comments about being with me but nothing is official. We do not even live together. Danielle's wedding will be a good indicator. In the meantime I must go kill a bunch of people to pass the time.

Just a little run in

Russia is always nice; I have always liked the culture and people. Blending in makes it easier because sometimes they are not so kind to outsiders. Luckily for me I can be anyone. Siberia was pleasant, the bed and breakfast I stayed made the best brown bread. I am not sure what the translation would be but it was delicious and the butter the homeowner made was to die for I could have eaten it by itself. As I started to track down Mr. Mystery Man I noticed it was taking me closer and closer to the guys. When I realized how close they where I started to listen in again.

Currently they had a similar lead to myself and where interviewing a couple people about Mr. MM. The Kid was a bit depressed this trip, though he was driven to find who was trying to kill him he really missed Elle and his girls. He hated to be away during these times especially now the baby was so small. He didn't want to miss any of her firsts espcecially when they are little and every day is something new and wonderful. Doc was focused at the task at hand, which helped the other guys and that is what gots him through until he gets home to Madison.

I liked to hear how Eric talked about me. Boomer and him were as close as ever though I am glad Eric did not go into details about our love life. The guys had been giving him a hard time on how fast he latched onto me and how cool I was about it. Dad seemed to be pessimistic that I was cool with the relationship because statistically we were doomed to fail though the Kid was fully supportive and thinks we will get married. Eric and Logan seemed to have the take 'when you know you know' and my relationship with Eric seemed to be so easy, it was almost too good to be true. From what I have seen, the ugly and bad, I am hesitant but I have always listened to my gut and I believe Eric and I have something special. I am going to enjoy the ride however long it lasts.

I could tell Boomer was supportive of Eric and I but he seemed aloof. I think he wants a relationship too but cannot let his heart free to try. I have a feeling I just caught Eric at the right time. Boomer is a family man, dedicated to his sister's kids and his mom and dad. I believe once he meets the right one the will devote to her. I could be wrong and he may end up being a man whore the rest of his life, as long as he is happy.

I think some hobo chic lady would do Dad wonders. He is so uptight I can't imagine him working with someone like himself. Like the TV show Darma and Greg. Eric mentioned once bunking with him and everything had a place. The bathroom sink was so orderly Eric was afraid to touch anything or even brush his teeth.

I was so close to the guys I wish we could have met up for some beers. Their interrogation lead them to me. I am currently staying in the building in which Mr. MM is supposedly at. I have been doing recon on every person in this place, from the staff to the guest. I have an overview of everyone that is in the blocks surrounding as well. Background checks and the staff all seem to be in order. As for the guest, there are so many I am making my way one at a time.

The guys have started to check into the guests as well, therefore I have had to stop my investigation to ensure they will never find me. Just a sweet divorcee looking to explore the world now that she is free from the terrible man that held her down, and I know they will never see me. Dad and Doc where on their computers and I was tracing everything they where doing. I was double dipping in what they where coming up with so we both did not have to do the same work.

Eric and Boomer where going to be arriving the in lounge in about twenty minuets to do a walk trough and get a feel for the layout and as some questions. I made sure to cover my tracks with hotel security and anyone else they may be able to identify me. This was not a normal Marine mission but someone higher up was giving them the okay. I feel like we could all be in an episode of Hawaii 5-0.

Eric and Boomer where dressed in street clothes and COM'd in to Richard. Eric looked so good; I am having a hard time with self-control right now. As they are talking to the Front Manager I brush by Boomer and place a tracking, listening sensor in his pocket. I don't have the guts to do it to Eric. I am too scared he would know, like get a vibe. I notice when I walk by he checks me out. I get kind of jealous then realize I cannot be jealous of myself. I make my way out of the hotel to the café down the road. This town is wonderful, a place to grab a snack and people watch. I notice that Richard has the same plan, I find him sitting on the patio sidewalk closest to the street. I hang back inside by the window where I have a clear view and click on my computer to track the guys.

They go with the manager to the room in question. They say they are looking for their brother and are very worried he has abandoned his family and gone on a bender. Apparently that is a symptom that crosses races, cultures and borders. It is a universal sign of despair that the manager seems very concerned about.

Upon entering the room the guys notice the smell immediately and know what they are going to find. The manager on the other hand has the surprise of his life waiting. They enter the bedroom to find a body. Looks to be the description of the man we have all been looking for but the guys and myself know that it is all too much of a conscience. I forward the information to Sir. The guys did the leg work for me. Helps me stay off the radar.

Before I COM off I hear the room maid mention the Ghost is back. This peeked Eric and Boomers interested. Sorry boys this one is not me.

Ghost Stories

I got a new hit a couple days later and I was on it. I tracked down the information source Sir found and was ready to extract information. I set up the room and waited, he arrived seven minuets late. I hate tardiness. These thugs have no consideration for others time. Feeling a little pent up with the dead body situation and probably being away from Eric I was not so nice to this guy.

He never saw me; he thought he was alone in the room with a computer communicating with someone who did not want to be found. Sadly for him I was in the connecting room and he was going to die once I got the information I needed. He talked and talked about different men he would send girls and children too. He gave dates, times and places. The money I offered with the comfort of the room I set up had him signing like a morning bird.

The voice conversation was being relayed straight to Sir in real time. Once he was done talking I chimed in with a couple more questions. I know he was not giving us the information we wanted and for some reason beating around the person we really wanted. With some blind threats to his family and more money he gave up three names that sparked Sir. I was given the sign we were done; I cleaned up, packed up and left.

The local police would not find the body for weeks or until someone walked into this shit hole and smelled is rotting body. The police would just rule it another gang killing. There was a thug group here that killed a certain way. Was easy to copy and I know they would take credit for it to save face in the cool/ tough category. Like shooting fish in a barrel.

Sir will be looking into the men located closer to him and in the States. There is one here I am looking into. Listening in on the guys one night I hear they are about to track down one of the associates of my mark, interesting. I make sure I coordinate with them so there is no overlapping and or running into each other.

Me: "Boys it is me"

Richard: "State your name this is a secure line."

Me: "This is Angel. Richard please check your computer for some helpful information. Stay Safe boys."

Replaying the conversation over in my head I found it interesting Richard asked if I was the Ghost. Rumors have spread across Europe over the years but only among the ones who know what is going on, and in the smaller superstitious towns. When I did not respond I think he let it go like he was more scared of the Ghost than he was of the evil men he worked for.

Back to reality I arrive early to find my target in a meeting with six other men, one being the man the guys are coming for. As the guys approach I realize they do not have all the information and are not prepared for the men present and the firearms and ammo they are packing. I COM into them.

Me: "Angel here boys, there are six men inside with enough firepower to take out the hotel your staying at. You where not suppose to show up for another hour."

Boomer: "What the fuck, we got new intel about twenty minuets ago?"

Me: "I have been watching them it's a set up. You could take them out in a fist fight but not with what they are packing."

Doc: "So what's the plan? How should we proceed?"

Me: "Turbo and Boomer should approach as planned, act as buyers, play the rouge men. I am set up to assist and take out any one coming in or out. Doc stay put and be the lookout. Richard, you need to move down to the bakery and order a tea. You need to make sure we do not have incoming visitors from the west end. Kid and Dad you need to take the back just in case. There is a staircase that leads right to the men from the back door. This access is never used and mostly blocked by bushes and trash so no one ever worries about that entrance and it is not guarded."

Richard: "I like this plan, do you have enough ammo in case this goes south?"

Me: "I always come prepared sir."

Turbo: "Thank you for watching over us."

Me: "Always here to help when I can."

God I missed that man. I hope it all goes smooth so I can question my guy. I have no clue how this will go but the extra men being there with all that ammo was unexpected. I have been trying to get a signal inside. I only need one of the men to turn thier cell phone on and I can hack into it and listen to everything. I keep scanning until I find it.

They are talking about stealing a shipment. They are actually going to take on the one calling the shots and steal the next shipment so they can make profit off these girls. Blonde and blue eyes brings in the big bucks and they want a payday, a visit from Eric and Boomer might lead to panic. I try to call they guys off but it is too late. These guys are high on something and not thinking straight. I think my target was trying to play both sides and double dip.

The scene played out like in a movie, bad guys are having a secret meeting, there is a knock at the door, there is suspicion, they forgot about the potential buyer of two new characters enter the building. There are a lot of questions, there is panic, the young, ghetto inexperienced bad guy makes a move and all hell breaks loose. I could not see faces but I watched the heat signatures.

Kid and Dad took shots fired as their signal to move and that, they did. I was able to take one guy out from my perch but I could not get a clear shot on anyone else. And without a clear eye on who it may be I was not going to take any chances with my guys being in there.

Doc: "Angel what's the status?"

Me: "Hold, the boys seem to be making a retreat."

From what I could tell Boomer and Turbo where returning fire from a side room and Kid and Dad where returning fire from the stare case. Not one seemed to be able to move or advance. I shot through the window knowing I would not hit anyone but hoping to get some movement and a line of sight. I know the guys could not hold them off based on their rounds but who was counting.

Richard: "I'm moving in Angel. Tell me my point of entry."

Me: "Go right in the front, go fast and hard, shooting the whole way."

Richard: "Copy."

And with that, guns blazing Richard was living out his wild west dreams. He kicked in the door shooting at nothing in particular but causing enough chaos to get the guys out of there. Turbo and Boomer where able to make it behind him and then without a signal they all turned and ran. That was my signal to start shooting and that is what I did. Kid and Dad made it out and down the block. Once I knew they where safe I cleaned up and headed out.

Unfortunately, no one got their man. All men in the building where dead and it was being ruled another gang incident. All of them had been wanted for something else so it was ruled as a deal gone bad before the crime scene was even cleaned.

Checking in on the guys I found out that Richard took a bullet in the side and the leg. He ran out of there fast for an old guy little alone a wounded one. Kid and Dad where a bit bruised from barreling out of the building and through the back and Boomer got a couple grazed shots and Eric took one to the arm. My heart stopped a second listening in on his status. I'm sure its nothing but that was too close a call for everyone.

Me: "Boomer how is everyone?"

Boomer: "Still coming down off the high. Thanks for the backup."

Me: "Glad to help when I can."

Boomer: "Have you been following us?"

Me: "No, just keeping tabs. We were looking for associates."

Boomer: "Was your guy meeting our guy?"

Me: "Yes."

Boomer: "So we both failed."

Me: "I don't use the term failed, just need to look elsewhere now."

Boomer: " We have been hitting road block after road block."

Me: "I know, I am trying to help. I have a lead that I will pass along if it pans out. But in the mean time no more meetings with the enemy please?"

Boomer: "What do you do when you are not saving our asses?"

Me: "Saving other asses."

Boomer: "We heard a story about you from one of the locals. I remember you referred to yourself as a ghost."

Me: "Yes, I have a different relationship with others."

Boomer: "You mean the Fucks of the world, you kill them."

Me: "Yes."

Boomer: "You will always be our Guardian Angel."

Me: "Thanks, I will always try to be."

Doc: "Have you made any way with your other lead?"

Me: "No word yet Sir."

Doc: "Call me Doc."

Me: "Once I know, I will pass it along Doc."

Doc: "Copy."

Me: "Boomer, what story of the Ghost did you hear?"

Boomer: "There is more than one?"

Me: "There are many. All very chilling."

Boomer: "The old man behind the bar, looked like he was way past one hundred was talking to another old man about the Ghost being back, something about saving the children. When we asked him about the story he got very still and serious. He started out: Many years ago when I was a young man there was a gang as we call them, the gang would come through town causing trouble. The police could never do anything about it because they were protected some how. We never found out who would help such men. But when this gang would come into town children would go missing.

After a while there where fewer and fewer members, they would come into town and drink and talk about how one of their own would disappear and or end up dead and no one knew how or why. They started to question each other. Then one night one of the meanest of the men, the top dog came in with an attitude. He ordered one drink and passed out. Passed out dead. The old man was the bartender that night and he himself had drank from the same bottle. No one knows how he died but they suspect that someone had killed him for all the wrong he had done to the community and the community was not sad about it but it left a mark on the town.

As time has passed they have seen a flux of bad guys come through and over the years members of society would end up dead with no cause. They suspect the

Ghost, that the men dying for no reason where the ones allowing the bad stuff to happen to begin with.

The old man went on to say there have been a string of deaths in Russia and the Ghost is out and to be aware. They are not scared of the Ghost. They seem to fear him but at the same time are thankful for protecting their people."

Me: "I have heard that one too."

Boomer: "We heard a scary one in Spain. But I didn't connect it to you until you mentioned multiple stories. If you are that deadly I really hope never to meet you in person."

Me: "I would never hurt you."

Boomer: "I wont take any chances. I am thankful for all you have done for us but if the stories are true we can just be pen pals."

Me: "May be we have already met."

Boomer: "Your scaring the shit out of me."

Me: "Oh shut up."

There are a couple stories about me that are so far fetched but fitting:

According to locals on Baltra Island, the former American Air Force base is haunted by "La Gringa sin Cabeza" or " Headless Gringa". Legends say that an American serviceman and his cheating wife live at the base during World War II. The soldier pushed his wife off a cliff when he found out she was cheating on him and her head got caught on something and tore off. Her ghost is said to target single men late at night by either ambushing them or killing them in their sleep. I heard a couple guys talking about this story one night. They were saying that it was actually the solider who was cheating and killed his wife to get out of his marriage. She stalks the nigh and kills deceiving men, that's why so many of the sinful guys around town end up dead.

La llorona, or *The Weeping Woman*, is about a Mexican woman who married a rich Spaniard. After they had children, the Spaniard lost interest in his wife and was embarrassed to be married to a woman without prestige. The woman then took all of her children to the river and drowned them thinking that would appease the Spaniard, but she was instantly hit with regret. She started screaming "Mis hijos, mis hijos," which means "*My children, my children*."

I have been called La llorona once by one nasty guy many years ago. He had a wine cellar full of children to use as he saw fit. Legends are very big in South America and while at the local market an old woman told him I was coming for him. She knew what he did and what a bad person he was. No one ever did anything about it, they where too scared of his level in society. So to make things more dramatic, it was in my college years, I scared the hell out of the children one night. They were by far more scared of him than me but when he went down to grab one for his pleasures they were all in a craze. Crying "the woman of the river was there."

This sent him into a panic so I played out my torture over the next twenty-four hours. I would release one child at a time into the forest to escape. As his guards reported the missing children he became even more frantic locking himself in his study. So, I naturally focused in on my inner Twilight Zone and snuck into the house setting off alarms.

Many of the guards took off at that point but the ones who stayed I had fun with them too. Long story short, as I looked into his eyes before he died he whispered La llorona. Not even a sorry, these people do not deserve to be on this earth. But I am not the one to judge.

Shaved Ice

Getting home I decompress for a couple days before I head back into the world. I clean and file everything away at the office and home then head off to some spa relaxation Danielle scheduled for us. She knows I am always tired from my travels but she just thinks it is because the flights are long and the food is bad. After my work trips sometimes I just have to turn the noise of the world off for a bit and stare off into space. Most people need therapy, I work out and give my worries to God.

That may sound super religious but when I first started out my dad told me if you cannot do anything about it give it to God, so I have ever since. And because of this I handle my stress and experiences quite well. I think having Danielle in my life helps too. She is my dose of reality.

Today we are going somewhere in Burlingame. I always love driving through Hillsborough to get there. I love all the big beautiful houses. If it wasn't a dead give away I would buy one, but people would question where I got my money. I love the land and ability to have my own little fortress. Like a lethal princess, with her secret dungeon of weapons. A girl can dream.

I get a picture text of Ululani's from Eric with:

This is my favorite spot on earth, the place I met you

He's laying it on thick. Four months away from each other is finally coming to an end. We will see how we are, either love birds that can't be away from each other or total awkwardness. I have been reading to many articles on service men and their wives/ relationships. It is a downer, so I am glad Danielle is talking my ear off about how great Eric is and how her and Matt think we are made for each other.

I get a couple other picture messages from Boomer and Dad of them all eating their shaved ice. I notice my dad is in one of the pictures. It throws me, first I thought my dad was still in Asia and second when did he become one of the boys?

Me: *Hey what's my dad doing with you guys?*

I love you too

Me: *I love you, I wish I could have made it to welcome you home*

Next time and I invited your dad

Me: *Why?*

We are in town and I wanted to catch up

Me: *Catch up with my dad? About what?*

Nothing you need to worry about

Me: *If I could I would spy on you right now*

I'll call you later babe, have fun with Danielle

How did he know I was with Danielle? When I asked Danielle she got all distracted with the road all of a sudden. No offense but I have been riding passenger with

Danielle since I was sixteen and not once has she ever paid attention to anything around her, and that is why her dad bought her a SUV when she got her license and Matt insisted on her getting a Denali for safety reasons. And when I started to question why Eric invited my dad it was like she did not even hear me.

Danielle is terrible about keeping secrets and I think she is really trying hard to keep something from me by evading my every concern. We make it to the spa in time for her to completely ignore my issues and get us checked in and separated. I have a nice massage and body scrub wrap. Danielle and I get a light lunch and do a little shopping before heading back.

Once home I call and leave a message for Eric then my dad. I wanted to see how shaved ice went, being that they went without me. I also am self loathing because I really wanted to be the good girlfriend and be waiting for Eric to get off the plane and run to me when he got home but they changed all the guys return flights being they got injured. So to add insult to injury I was not there for my wounded boyfriend to arrive safely home.

With that rant out of my system and my body being Jello from today's spa treatments I pass out, no TV or anything. I wake up the next morning with a couple miss calls and texts. Two missed calls from Eric and a text: *hello?* And one text from my dad: *be home in the afternoon.*

When Eric and I finally talk he tells me about shaved ice and the sunset. They guys did not feel right not having me there. Even though it is an ode to their Angel, me being there the first time signified something for them. Now I am feeling bad again. Eric tells me my dad was cool. Really? He told old war stories but he got weird when Doc asked my dad if he had ever heard the legends of the Ghost.

Eric: "He got quiet and just nodded. Like he knew the stories too well. The stories are Robin Hood like but have a scary mystery to them."

Me: "Yeah I have heard my dad talking to other Marines in the past about those stories."

Eric: "Its inspiring that there is someone out there riding the world of evil. From what we heard it is some one that mostly kills of the bad guys who harm women and children."

Me: "Oh wow. I guess someone has to protect them."

Eric: "For a long time we all thought it might be you."

Me totally nervous: "What?"

Eric: "Well you did show up the day we went to honor Angel and then your dad showed you off as this master of arms. We all had our suspicions. But Boomer thinks you are too soft for that."

Me: "Thanks Boomer."

Eric: "But if you were I would be cool with it. I have always wanted to date Wonder Woman."

Me laughing: "Your stupid."

Eric: "Well we know it can't be you because the stories go back fifty years or more. You were not even alive."

Me: "Can I still get a Wonder Woman costume then?"

Eric: "Stop, your killing me. This is torture. Your so close yet so far away."

Me: "Why don't you just come in earlier for Danielle's wedding, and stay longer; if you want."

Eric: "I like the way you think."

We talked about the Kids little girls and how the baby has grown. Eric was in awe of the difference four months made. It was sweet to hear him talk like that. Like may be we could have a life together. That is some thing I hope to talk to my own dad about. I know he should be getting in any time, so we will see.

A talk with Dad

Sir came just in time for dinner. He made a stop at the office in which I was alerted and knew he would come see me right after. When he comes to visit he tends to sleep in the dungeon and not one of my remodeled guest rooms. We have a nice meal before he dives into his findings.

Sir: "There is unrest above us. Someone has taken the ghost stories seriously and has been trying to track down a person to link all the killings over the last hundred years. It seems to be believed it is an American or Russian, and who ever is leading the hunt got conformation when you saved those Marines. Apparently, they wanted to take the Marines out for wreaking the shipment a couple years ago. They lost millions in children, ammo and God know what else. All twenty-five soldiers are tied to the financial destruction or loss of some kind in regards to this trafficking group. Looks like someone wanted to round them up and kill them for what they did. This group spans the world."

Me: "But not all of us are American."

Sir: "No one knows that though. There are branches around the world. Back in the day we had assignments together, but now with how information is collected it is easier and safer for us to work alone."

Me: "Was China a bust?"

Sir: "No it lead me to a couple other people that have been on our hit list for years."

Me: "Years? Why where they not handled sooner?"

Sir: "Some are left to continue as a lead to others. There is been people that have been able to hide in the shadows like us. Most are already on our radar but we do not hunt without proof."

Me: "Understandable. How was Eric and the guys?"

Sir: "Going to Ululani's really helps. That was a good suggestion to them. Some times it is hard to heal and continue regular life after some of the things we go through. I used to worry about you, some how you where gifted with a duty gene. If it is your duty you are able to let it be."

Me: "That sounds about right."

Sir: "So things with you and Eric are serious?"

Me: "I think they are moving in that direction."

Sir: "How will you proceed?"

Me: "I am not sure, do I tell him? Do I hide this forever? And what about marriage and kids? I do want a family someday, how does that play into all this?"

Sir: "You take it how it comes and there is always work around's. There have been members that have taken years off and come back better than ever. It is a life mission you never leave. But you are able to make your own hours and apply certain restrictions. You can make it work."

Me: "Okay, I guess we will wait and see."

Sir: "Investing in properties has helped me. You can have a dungeon anywhere."

Me: "Who knows we do not even live together yet. Hiding a secret room may be hard."

Sir: "How many times has he stayed here and he has no idea. Danielle practically lived here one summer and does not know. You did not find out until I showed you."

Me in deep thought: "True"

Sir: "I took some time off after I retired from the Marines. But once a Marine always a Marine and I needed to do something. So I hit it hard when you guys where little, backed off a bit as you got older then dedicated myself to your training while you where in high school. When I became your handler I realized I could spend more time with your mother. When she passed away I went one hundred percent for a year then scaled it back. You have always made it work for your life style and can continue. I am just glad you found something else to occupy your life. I never wanted this to consume you. I have always wanted it all for you."

Me: "I think Eric wants to stay in Hawaii. That is where his family is."

Sir: "It is important for him to be with those guys, they are his family. His mom and dad are very important but his brothers give him life."

Me: "Too bad he couldn't just help me with my assignments, I know that is far fetched."

Sir: "There was a husband wife couple when I was younger."

Me: "What happened to them?"

Sir with a distant look in his eyes: "They had children."

Me: "Children change everything."

Sir laughing: "Just you wait."

During Sir's stay we talk a lot about family and how he and my mom made things work. They had a strong relationship, totally committed to each other so the other stuff just fell into place. My mom knew of his gun obsession and accepted early on that he had to travel for work. Being he provided for his family nothing ever came up. The really worked as a couple and having kids they made a plan to have my mom stay home and raise us until we went to school. Then she went back to work at the church. I am not sure if that is always what she did but she was happy to be active in our lives.

I know once Sir officially retired and we were all out of the house mom and dad traveled a lot. I really thought it was to see the world together but for some reason I cannot shake the feeling I am missing something.

I actually stay up late that night lost in my own thoughts. I would love a family but I really do not know how to make it work. Technically, financially I do not need to work ever again. I have done well for myself. But I know in my heart I cannot stop helping others. I guess the one thing about life it is unpredictable and learning to just enjoy the ride is my current goal in life.

Bringing kids into the world is a scary thought, especially knowing there could be an attack at any time. Nine Eleven was an eye opener for me. Eric and I did talk about that day and what it meant to the both of us. He woke up to his mom and dad being home. They usually were both dressed and bolting out the door yelling at him to get ready. That day they let him sleep in and stayed home with him. They day after was a day of chaos for the Military community. He will never forget the smells, they look in peoples eyes and his parents response. He knew then he wanted to be just like them.

As for me, things were a little different at my house. My parents kept us home from school that day. My mom did call my grandmother to come stay with us as her and my dad needed to go and check on their New York Property Real Estate. My mom came home a week later and my dad went to Los Angelas to take care of business. He flew home on the weekends, holidays and if we had anything important going on.

I remember people being afraid and scared. I told myself that day that I never wanted to feel that way again. I never wanted to be scared, helpless or unable to protect myself. I guess it has always been inside me to do what I do. People are just born a certain way. I know who I am.

Eric gets serious

Eric had been awkward on the phone lately. I have a feeling he is trying to tell me something then our conversation gets side tracked. Danielle's wedding is coming up and I worry that he may be having second thoughts about being my date. Being an amateur at dating I realize I am just stressed out and freaking out.

Eric: "Are your ready for me?"

Me: "What are you wearing? Do I need to pick you up a suit?"

Eric: "I got it taken care of. How are you?"

Me: "Good. I think I have everything done. Just have to deal with Danielle and all her last minuet things."

Eric: "No I mean are you okay?"

Me: "Yeah why wouldn't I be?"

Eric: "You have been a little off when we talk lately."

Me: "I could say the same about you."

Eric: "Really? You have never given me attitude before."

Me: "Sorry. I just feel like there is something you are not telling me."

Eric: "I don't want to fight with you."

Me: "This isn't a fight."

Eric: "I don't like it though."

Me: "Me either."

Eric: "I know it has been forever since we have seen each other but it will be okay. We are good."

Me: "Okay."

Eric: "Your making being away from you even harder with your tone."

Me: "Sorry I just feel like I am missing something and I am usually five steps ahead and with you I feel five steps behind in a dark closet."

Eric: "You have nothing to worry about."

Me: "Okay"

Eric: " Seriously I love you more than you know."

Me: "I love you too."

Eric: "Please stop."

Me: "Stop what?"

Eric: "Just because I can's see you I know the face your making."

Me with a smile now: "Do you really think you know me that well?"

Eric: " I think I know you better than anyone. Inside and out."

Me: "Whatever perv."

Eric: "At least I got you to laugh."

Me: " Will you just get here already."

Eric: "Soon enough. But are you ready for me this time?"

Me: "Yes"

Eric: "Are you going to come back with me still after the wedding?"

Me: "Yes, you know this already."

Eric: "Just checking."

Me: "What's going on? You have asked me that every time we have talked this week."

Eric: "Nothing I just want to make sure."

Me: "I may not be able to see you but now I know something is up. What is going on?"

Eric: "Nothing really. I wanted to see you in person to talk about it."

Me: "What is going on? Are you going to break up with me? If so you should just do it now and not even bother coming to Danielle's wedding."

Eric: "GOD NO! No way."

Me: "Then why all the weirdness?"

Eric: "I just want to ask you to move in with me but wanted to ask you in person so I could gage your reaction."

Me: "Are you afraid I will say no?"

Eric: "I just know you have been in the Bay Area all your life. Danielle said you would say yes and your dad was excited about it. But I don't know."

Me: " Well I guess you will never know unless you ask."

Eric after a frustrated sigh: "Will you move in with me?"

Me after a long pause: "Yes. Is that why you mentioned we should look at houses for fun?"

Eric: "Yes. I thought we could find something that is just ours."

Me: "I would like that. I have a lot of needs."

Eric: "Yeah I know, tell me about it."

And with that the awkwardness was gone. He had been dodging the question and I think was glad it was over. I got on Zillow later that night and looked around at places. I was not sure what price range he would be ok with so I started to look at fixer uppers. That way we could have a nice place and I can add some important necessities.

Sadly I see nothing on Zillow I like under two million. I know that may be scary for Eric so I will have to see how house hunting goes. There is one I really like in Kailua Bay off Kalaheo Avenue which is close to the base and has a lot of privacy for me to make a couple additions.

I switch off my computer and am glad the awkwardness is gone. I do not know why I jumped the gun and stressed out. I should know better. I am just in unknown waters and learning to swim. Danielle has been a big help, even though I am kind of mad at her for not giving me a heads up Eric talked to her about wanting me to move in with him. I know it was a concern of his when he came to the shower but I figured we would just work it out when we got there. We are there now.

The Wedding

My Maid of Honor dress was nice, sexy to be exact. It flattered my figure. It is a deep navy blue, floor length, form fitting and Eric loved it. I spent the most of the wedding day with Danielle, hair, and makeup. Eric swung by a few times to bring me coffee, lunch and to steal a couple kisses. He went golfing and did his own thing. But when he saw me come out of the room in my dress he looked as though he might pass out. I took that as a good sign. Win for me.

Getting ready with Danielle and the girls we shared stories of her and Matt. There was a time in Middle school that we were all in the quad, Matt and Danielle just started to date and where kissing at the picnic tables when one of the lunch monitors came over and told them to break it up. We all went wild with laughter and they where so embarrasses. One pumpkin festival we all roller bladed around. We knew the back streets and tried to avoid the crowd but one afternoon Danielle had to have another piece of pumpkin pie and the stand was in front of the I.D.E.S. hall on Main Street, so of course Matt bladed over, through the crowd to get her a piece only to return with it stuck to the front of his shirt. It was so adorable. Poor guy didn't even care and left the stain on his shirt the rest of the day. Angela shared a story of when Matt tried to set me up with one of his friends at our eight grade dance and when I realized what was happening and totally ran away Danielle let him have it. Even though Danielle initially thought it was a good idea she had my back even then. Matt knew is place after that. I think he was just trying to be nice so I wasn't the third wheel but I did not handle it well. I called my mom to come get me and bailed on everyone. Looking back it was funny and I kind of feel bad for his poor friend.

When he first got into town it was a little awkward with the aftermath of the living together conversation but all was cleared up once we made time for each other after dinner. We seemed to fall right back into place which made me feel better about our relationship. I was the one being awkward so I have no one to blame but myself. It was like I was on my period or something. I don't know why I was being so weird about it.

Eric walked up to me slowly taking me in. He placed his arms around me and gave me a long, deep kiss. It was an intense kiss. I think we were progressing in our relationship faster and faster these last couple of days. At the rehearsal dinner he didn't take his eyes off of me. He had no idea what was going on around us. It made me a little nervous at first but then I totally fell for it. Danielle made a comment that we were next and it didn't even faze him. Eric and I were beginning to be a regular staple in this town.

Eric drove me over to the Our Lady of the Pillar Church because Danielle was riding over with her parents in her Uncles Jaguar. It was total silence during our drive. When we pulled into the parking lot we sat for a moment before Eric spoke.

Eric: "You look amazing."

Me: "Thank you"

Eric: "No really, it hurts my insides with how good you look."

I just stayed quiet because I was so shy and really unable to comprehend someone actually though of me that way.

Eric: "I love you."

Me: "I love you too."

Eric: "Today is a lot."

Me: "That is Danielle."

Eric just looked over at me and smiled. I knew everything was okay but in the moment I felt the heaviness of our relationship progressing. We have only known each other less than a year but the time spent together and apart have been the best eight months of my life. I realized sitting in the car with him that today was a major turning point for us. Moving in together was just the first step to what was to come.

Silence spoke volumes when it came to Eric and I. We didn't have to talk. Being next to each other was pure electricity that was hard to control sometimes. I made the move to get out of the car when he grabbed my arm and kissed me. I finally had to pull away because if I didn't I don't think we would have made it to the ceremony.

One of the bridesmaids was having a moment. The rehearsal dinner meal she picked was not sitting well with her for the last couple hours and she was starting to panic that it was getting worse. Danielle told her to stay in the bathroom until it was game time then after she could retreat back. I think she was going to be fine once she got it all out. What's a wedding without a little drama?

Walking up the isle I made eye contact with Eric. He was smiling ear to ear. Nothing in that moment mattered but the two of us. Being born and raised in this town this church symbolized my youth, my growing up catholic with my catholic friends. The boy in youth group I liked but didn't notice me. This church was where we came as a family for Sunday services and Holidays. It was also the place where we celebrated my mom's life. Eric really had no idea what this place was to me.

Danielle made her way down the isle in the perfect white princess dress. She looked like Geisel from Enchanted. Matt's reaction was picture perfect and I was loving every second. Taking a glance in the crowd I noticed my dad slipped in next to Eric. I did not know he was going to be here. Then again Danielle was like another daughter to him. Growing up we where inseparable.

Eric mouthed I love you so naturally I had to mouth it back. Sir gave me a look then smiled. The vows were standard and when Danielle and Matt kissed the crowd went wild. I realized I was getting teary eyed but managed to keep it together.

Walking out of the church at the end Eric grabbed my arm and held me in the hallway off to the side of the church. He held me close and buried his face in the nape of my neck. I will never tire of that. It is one of my favorite things.

Eric: "I don't want this day to end."

The reception was beautiful. Danielle and Matt made their grand entrance and I could tell she was the happiest she has ever been. I sat back to take it all in. The colors, the smells, the people. There will never be a gathering of these people ever again. Weddings seem to bring people together and it was beautiful.

Sir: "You look beautiful daughter."

Me: "Thanks Dad. I am glad you came."

Sir: "Eric looks at you like Matt looks at Danielle."

Me: "I know."

Sir: "I am happy for you. Don't be scared to go for it."

It was time for my Maid of Honor speech and I was so nervous. I have never been the center of attention and especially with this group of people.

"My speech is mainly for Danielle. I know Matt may understand some of it but being that Danielle is my long lost sister we have a bond that is hard to describe. You are the most passionate person I know. Matt you do not know the dedication and unconditional love you have married. She is fierce and protective. She will fight the world for you. The joining of your kind love and sweet heart will make your life together one for the books. You have changed the world as we know it with your unity and I am looking forward to witnessing the greatness you bring the world. You ain't never had a friend like me, but I am glad Matt is trying."

Danielle burst into tears and so did I. People clapped but only Matt really understood. I think Eric caught on too. Up until this day it was Danielle and I. Now it is Danielle and Matt. I have to say that I am so happy for her because I know things wont really change. Matt knows he is getting me as a sister now and that no matter what her and I will be close. I think the only one that knows me as well as Danielle is Eric and that makes this transition okay for me.

Eric while we dance: "Will you fight the world for me?"

Me: "Yes."

Eric: "I would die for you."

Me: "Please don't."

Eric: "So Robin Hood can't be our romantic movie we compare our life too?"

Me: "Why that movie?"

Eric: "Because he is a tuff handsome guy that falls for a tough beautiful woman. Remember she fights him in the beginning of the movie?"

Me: "As you wish."

Eric: "Don't make fun of me but I know that's from Princess Bride."

Me: "I like movies and books. They are a great escape."

Eric: "But you have me now, you don't need any of that."

Me: "Well I guess I will only keep a couple books then when we move in together. Wouldn't want to clutter up the place with literature."

Eric: "You saying that is music to my ears."

Eric lays a kiss on me and we dance in our own little love bubble. When it is time for cake we are ready to sit down. We slow danced to every song. It was kind of funny to see people's reactions to us just doing our own thing. Danielle' cake was so yummy. Eric asked if he would get a say in our cake.

Me: "It will be fifty percent your wedding so you can make half the decision but we must both agree."

Eric: "Will that be your wedding dress then?"

Me: "More than likely not."

Eric: "Please keep it."

Me: " I like when you wear all black. The night of the bachelorette I have hammered into my brain."

Eric: "As you wish."

The entire night was filled with smiles and laughs. Eric and I managed to spend most of the time together. There were a few moments when I had to break away for best friend duties. When it came time to toss the bouquet I was not planning to go up but Danielle, Matt and Eric all ganged up on me. Talk about peer pressure. I think Danielle aimed right at me because I caught it and the crowd went wild. Eric just smiled and winked at me. He didn't end up catching the garter belt but Matt's friend Brandon from middle school did. Him and I took some pictures together and I went back to Eric's side.

My feet where starting to hurt but I know I looked good so I powered through. While dancing Eric was practically caring me the whole time so it worked out in my favor. The night was magical for Eric and I and I thank Matt for finally make it happen with Danielle. Everything happens the way it is suppose to.

We stayed until the end then made our way home. He carried me through my front door and straight to the bedroom. Not speaking a word he took off my dress and laid me in bed. There are no words to describe what happened next. We didn't speak to one another but got lost in each other.

Eric: "Everything about the wedding was Grand. The attention to detail was impeccable."

Me: "Danielle leaves no stone unturned."

Eric: "Your speech was perfect."

Me: "Thanks I was nervous about it."

Eric: "There was not a dry eye in the house."

Me: "What do you mean, it wasn't much."

Eric: "But everyone knows how much you two mean to each other. It wasn't a goodbye but I couldn't be more proud of you type of speech. People got it."

Me lost in though: "Good."

Eric: "Matt's speech to Danielle was great too. He knows she is a handful and he actually is excited about it. Like bring it on. He is tougher than people give him credit for."

Me: "He really is a good person. I am glad it worked out between them after all these years. They are really perfect for each other."

Eric: "You think that about us?"

Me: "Yes. Do you?"

Eric: "Soul mates."

Me: " Now you're just being mushy."

Eric: "I was so nervous to ask you to move in with me. I was so afraid you would say no."

Me: "What made you think that?"

Eric: "You have a life. You have a job, friends, and a house. You just met me while on vacation. I was just afraid if you said no that I missed something."

Me: "I had a life before you but I like my life with you in it better."

Eric: "I needed to hear that."

Me: "But I know you are going to be gone for long periods of time so when we find a place can I make it ours with some added things to help me pass the time while you are gone?"

Eric: "Like what?"

Me: "Like a library. Or a very large book shelf?"

Eric: "I could live with that. Do you know what you are going to bring over with you?"

Me: "My clothes and my bed spread set if that's okay with you?"

Eric: "Yeah I love your bed."

Me: "Its actually our bed because I bought it right before you came to visit the first time."

Eric: "Perfect. But your not going to bring any furniture?"

Me: "No, Ill just leave my house here as is and let me family use it for vacations or trips out here. We can go shopping when we find a place and make it ours."

Eric: "We will need new dishes for sure."

This made me laugh. I had the worse set of dishware ever and after spending the day after the wedding with Danielle and Matt opening gifts Eric and I were making a list of all the things we wanted. I loved the Tiffany's tea set she got and Eric loved the brown recliner Matt got. They registered for a lot of stuff for their home because they still had not entirely moved in after they bought it. It was a renovation project that was still two years until completion.

One of Madison's friends is a Real Estate Agent on the island and she will be taking us around looking at homes. Eric gave me her email the day after I agreed to move in with him and have been corresponding with her ever since. I told her our wants and as for price I told her not to mention it to Eric. I can afford the homes we will be looking at on my own so no need to worry him with the finances.

With this whole process I have been shooting high. I want a pool and enough rooms to stay there forever if we get married and have kids. I will need to secure a dungeon somehow and do not want to make an investment I have to uproot and change in a couple years. I have not discussed this with Eric yet and really do not know how. I make a lot of money and do not want him to worry yet do not want to emasculate him. It's a fine line but I will get there when I get there.

The night before we are set to head to Hawaii Eric makes a loud thump in the hallway. He tripped on something on the floor. Thankfully he was caring a load of laundry so I told him I would take care of it. The dungeon's entrance door was ajar. Somehow it was cracked open and Eric caught his foot on it. I was able to close and secure it before Eric came back around. Was my dad over getting supplies while we were at the reception? I had to text him to make sure. My blood started to pump fast and my heart race.

Thankfully Sir responded immediately, which set me at ease. He came by to get things ready to head back to Hawaii and left without securing everything. He is so used to me not having company he forgot.

In my moment of panic I wondered what Eric would think if he found out. He has made a couple comments in the past that lead me to believe he would be okay with it. Like he knows I am Angel. I know I am flawless in covering my tracks but could we have such a connection that he just knows? That we could be soul mates? Is there even such thing? My initial panic turned into curiosity.

We pack up the house and set out to the airport. Traveling with Eric is easy but I am concerned about him looking into my luggage. I am used to traveling with a set of tools and I am not sure how he would react to learn about my travel tendencies. I know a Gloc in a purse can be explained but I have not traveled without my kit since before High School.

When Eric goes away

The flight was nice. I booked us first class on Hawaiian Airlines and Eric was grateful. Oddly it brought up a conversation I was not prepared for.

Eric: "So, you fly first class a lot?"

Me: "Always to Hawaii."

Eric uncomfortably: "Isn't it more expensive?"

Me: "Not much more. And for the long flight it is defiantly more comfortable."

Eric: "You do well at work don't you?"

Me: "Yeah, I think I am pretty good at what I do."

Eric: "I meant financially."

Me: "Oh, yeah. I was fortunate to take over my dad's clients and secure some of my own. These companies pay well."

Eric: "So, that makes you my sugar mama?"

Me: "If your okay with that? I have always just worked, made a good living and have not had many expenses. Never had much of a life outside of work until I met you either."

Eric: "You know Marines do not make much right?"

Me: "I don't love you for your money."

Eric: "I mean if we are going to get a place I do not have a lot to offer."

Me: "Do not worry about it. We will find something that works for the both of us."

Eric seemed to relax: "Okay"

Me: "If it makes you feel any better I will stay home with the children and you can go out and make a living for us."

Eric: "Shut up. I am just entering new territory with you. But I can handle. May be I will stay home with the kids and you can give us the life style we deserve."

Me: "If that's what you want."

I think it was weird for him to know I made a lot of money but in an odd way I think he was okay with it. He was raised with a mom and dad who where equals in rank, and pay grade so I do not think traditional gender roles effected him. But the fact he did not quite know how much I really made left him in limbo that we still had a lot to learn about each other.

Luckily if anyone where to ever run a credit check on me they would learn I make a lot of money but nothing close to what I actually have on hand. Sir helped me set up some off shore accounts and investments when I first started that have allowed me to make more money and secure my safety. I have enough in my savings to pay for our new home in cash.

When we land I grab our rental car and head to our hotel. We take it easy the rest of the day. We are both quiet, not talking much when Eric bluntly brings up our last conversation.

Eric: "I didn't mean to be weird about the money thing."

Me: "No worries. I never really thought about it before."

Eric: "I knew you did well for yourself and I do okay too. I have always saved my money. I know moving in together is a big step and certain things are going to come up."

Me: "Want to talk about them now before we get too deep?"

Eric: "It doesn't matter I want to be with you no matter what."

Me: "Want to get them out of the way then?"

Eric: "Sure. Lets do it."

Me: "So what do you want to know?"

Eric: "What price range of home are we looking into?"

Me: "How about I will buy it in both our names and you can pay the utility bills? Or you want specific numbers?"

Eric: "That works for me. Is there anything about you that might come as a shock?"

Me: "I do have a gun collection. I have been shooting since I was in High School and I do enjoy it. Can we have a weapon closet? Secured of course."

Eric: "I get that. Especially after seeing your dads place. I guess with a Marine dad I shouldn't expect anything less."

Me: "To be honest my sisters have them too. Even my little sister that is weapon adverse. My dad taught us to be able to protect ourselves."

Eric: "I figured that. I found your safe at your house."

Me: "And?"

Eric: "I figured it was because of your dad."

Me: "True. And what about you?"

Eric: "I like my weapons and I guess we should secure them just in case there is a break in or we have guests."

Little does he know there will never be a break-in. The level of security we will have will be beyond his knowledge or concern.

Me: "We have spent a lot of time together but is there any quirks you may have that I should know about?"

Eric: "Like what? I am a basic guy. I am not good a laundry but I clean up after myself."

Me: "You are not obsessed with porn or anything weird like that are you?"

Eric after a big laugh: "Oh God no. I am actually pretty boring. If it wasn't for you I would just read, watch movies or go on adventures hiking."

Me: "We could still do all of that. And if you want alone time I can accommodate you."

Eric: "I don't want alone time."

Me: "Okay"

Eric: "Do you think you would want children some day?"

Me surprised with such a heavy question: "Yes, I have only recently thought about it but yes."

Eric: "Would you want kids with me?"

Me: "I have only ever thought of my future since I have been with you."

This gets me a smile and I can see the tension in Eric leave. I am not sure why the intense questions over the last twelve hours but I guess this is what couples need to discuss if they want to be together. I know it's a good thing to get some of these awkward talks out of the way to make sure we are on the same page and want the same things. We have moved fast since we met and I am sure Eric is feeling vulnerable as am I. It feels so perfect to be together but money and kids are big issues for couples. If you do not have common goals or wants things can get tricky down the road.

Funny thing about this talk with Eric was that Danielle had given me this checklist back when we first met. It was the one hundred and twenty one questions to ask to get to know your guy. I laughed at first but thinking of it I had to share with Eric.

He thought it was funny but we spent the next couple hours going through the questions. Where were you born? What's your favorite color? Mine is green and Eric's is blue. What' s your favorite ice cream? If you had three wishes, what would they be? What's your favorite food? I already knew Eric's was steak and potatoes as is most males but he was surprised mine was sandwiches. We both already knew our coffee and drink preference but dream car made us laugh. Eric wants an old Bronco and I want an old Woody. He had some crude comments for me the rest of the night.

It was fun to go through the list and make a game of some questions we already knew and go over important things we should know about each other.

The next day we spent the afternoon with Elle and Logan and the girls. I was nice to finally see the baby and hang out with Elle. Her and I have become good friends since we met and spending time with her and her family was easy. No expectations. It was simple.

Seeing Eric with the girls was precious. I know he loves his parents very much but it wasn't until today that I realized how much he wanted a family of his own. I think he wants to be the man and father he never had himself. It was reassuring of my love for him. I think I made a good choice in opening my heart to him.

I was surprised in myself too. I was actually good with the girls, especially the baby. I never had much time with little ones and was scared to hold her at first but it was sweet. I think Eric liked it a lot because he never took his eyes off me the whole time I had the baby.

I feel like we have moved really fast and I know he loves me but I really hope he wants me for me and not just because he wants a family so bad he is willing to sign up with the first girl he can.

Elle must have sensed my concern because she called me out once the guys went inside for more beers.

Elle: "Don't worry. He loves you for you not that he wants to get married and have a family. He's not just filling some void."

Me: "What?"

Elle: "It's written on your face and I know him too well. He is the lover, sweetheart of the group. Things changed for him after he met you."

Me: "Really?"

Elle: "Yes, you're his world because he really loves you. And Marines tend to move fast. If it is too fast for you tell him. He will understand."

Me: "No, everything is going fine. I just have never had anyone notice me the way he has. Its all a little foreign to me."

Elle: "You do not see yourself in the right light. Your not as invisible as you think."

Her last comment makes me happy but uncomfortable. I have stayed alive because I am invisible. I do not take her comment as a good thing. What did that mean for me as a professional?

The next day was fun looking at houses with Eric. We looked at thirteen houses and only agreed on two of them. The one I liked the most was private, has a pool and generally does not need much work. It is close to the beach, which is nice, even though I really wanted something on the beach. Eric was a little concerned with the prices but I just told him it was about seeing what we each liked and wanted. My goal was to see what his wants where, see the things he had to have and what was on his wish list.

Me: "How far away from the base are you okay with living?"

Eric: "It is an island, the commute wont be bad no matter where we end up."

Me: "Are you sure? I loved the one in Laie but the one in Waialua was nice too. It reminded me of the house in Hawaii 5-0.

Eric: "I liked both of them but the one in Waialua is far. I would like to stay on this side of the island. I liked the one in Punaluu and Hauula but they seem like they are really expensive. I know Hawaii is not cheap."

Me: "Don't worry about the price. What my baby wants my baby gets."

Eric: "I feel like your turning me into a kept man."

Me: "A girl can only dream."

Eric: "You would like that wouldn't you?"

Me: "Yes, for me to use as I wish. Doesn't every girl want that?"

Eric: "What my baby wants my baby gets."

His send off was hard. Him leaving just keeps getting harder and harder. I know even when we move in together he will have to leave. I do not know how Elle and Madison do it. It is stressful. I have been alone for so long and now that Eric is apart of my life I am not so comfortable being alone.

I did the whole send off at the base. It was like in the movies. It was hard to finally say goodbye. He will be gone for about six months and I am not looking forward to it. I will be traveling back and forth to the bay and back until I finalize on the house and start construction. I already told Sir my plans and he is going to facilitate the construction of the dungeon and I will supervise the other upgrades.

Before any thing final is made I need to run it by Eric but the last couple days we have been too involved in each other to talk about anything else. We have been so consumed in one another that the rest of the world has not mattered. He has even ignored Boomer and Richard on some of their new findings. I think the reality of us being apart is finally setting in.

His send off is nothing grand. Other families are there to say goodbye for now. I notice that Dad has someone seeing him off which is nice. I am glad he found someone else besides his brothers to devote his time too. When Eric finally breaks away from me I can see the sadness in his eyes. This is really hard for him.

Eric: "The last time I left you were not here and it made it easier for me to get on that plane."

Me: "Sorry to make your life harder."

Eric: "Make it as difficult as you want. You are not getting rid of me."

Me: "Didn't plan on it."

Eric: "Will you be barefoot in the kitchen when I get back?"

Me: "As you wish."

Renovations

With Eric out on his Unit Deployment Program U.D.P. I contact the Real Estate agent and gave her the go on the house in Kailua Bay. It fits both of our wants and needs. When Eric called the first time after his departure he told me to pick, that he would love whatever I chose and he really didn't care as long as we were together.

Sir flew in for the inspection and to get an idea on how we were going to put in a dungeon. Though I cannot call it the dungeon any more so I tease my dad and tell him it is the paa mai. Which is Hawaiian for dungeon. He never liked me calling it the dungeon to begin with. He thought that it was more of a safe space not something to be associated with fear.

Being that it takes time for the paper work to go through and the people to move out I opted to head back to Half Moon Bay to get my life in order to move. I first went to the office and secured the back room. I know that Sir and I will be using my office as a mid destination for supplies and to lay low between jobs. Both of us being in Hawaii will mean we need to arrange our travel differently. I know I will be coming back and forth occasionally for work regardless but I want to make sure everything is in order.

As for my house there is too much to move. I will bring my clothes (not all of them because it is not cold in Hawaii) and my new comforter set. I think it is more cost effective to buy new stuff over there. I know Eric wants a recliner and an outdoor kitchen so I have already budgeted in that for our new place.

I have three more weeks until I can start construction so decided to take on some extra work to pass the time. Thankfully I just take a trip down south. I am able to drive across the border and road trip through Mexico through Guatemala to Costa Rica. It is a beautiful drive but extremely dangerous for a young girl on her own. I encounter a lot more than expected which adds to my already large numbers. While in Belize I tacked on the points, if this was a game I think in my first week I would have won.

Before Sir can get started on my construction project he follows up on some leads regarding the guys. We still have not been able to pin point anyone yet for the false Intel and the wild goose chase. Sir is getting frustrated. No one has ever been this hard for him to track down. I know he is getting help from high up. Hopefully we are not the only ones on this mission. I have a feeling it is just cleaning house while we get to who we need. I try to stay positive.

I know there is a couple guys in Europe that stay busy. I know a lot of the scary stories about Ghosts are about them. They are brutal killers. They like to leave a gruesome scene especially with the child molesters. From what Sir has told me about them they are brothers that lost their parents in a home invasion. Their father was involved in our organization and left the boys to his mentor upon his death. Apparently Sir had the same papers in place in case anything happened to him and my mom.

Being a parent comes with more to organize than I realized. Having kids is a huge undertaking. With Eric being gone so much if we were to have kids it would fall on me. I am sure I can handle it but it is still daunting to think about.

Taking my time south I make a couple out of the job stops. It is so beautiful here one can see why so many people live in these areas even though they are very dangerous. San Francisco is just as dangerous but easy to maintain. I guess no matter where you go you take the good with the bad. It is all what you can stand.

I spend the most time in Costa Rica. I love the food and the beaches. I also make a pit stop in Panama before heading home. I take a couple plane rides through the south before heading into Texas then home. It is sometimes easier to cross the border by car than by plane. Though LAX is the easiest place to travel through. There are so many flights and it is such a hub for people and celebrities the security is lax and I have personally see people slip in and out with out concern. With that I have taken upon myself to right securities wrong.

After nine eleven security was up tight but got relaxed again soon after. Even though it is said that LAX is the entry point for most criminals no one ever seems to fix the problem. Sir spent six months in Los Angeles after nine eleven. I think it changed everyone's outlook and sense of purpose.

When Eric calls I tell him I have a surprise for him when he gets back. I think he knows but plays coy. Via video chat I show him some designs to get his honest take on some of the decorating ideas I have in mind. I want to keep the home true to the Hawaiian plantation style it is but add some bold colors and modern wallpaper. I ask him if he wants all the stuff from his apartment and he gives me a list of what to keep and what to donate.

His apartment is actually nice for a bachelor pad. It is a one bedroom with a small kitchen and small bathroom. Really only meant for him. We stayed there a couple nights one time and it was not bad. It is not an actual apartment in a building but more of a small shed on some ones property they converted into a small guesthouse. The property has two of them. The family that lives in the main house is apart of the Marine Corps some ones house and the second apartment is vacant.

It is peaceful and I can see why Eric loved living there so much. The people keep to themselves and there are trees all around. Sitting outside on the mini patio one night you cannot hear a thing. It was tranquil. Something I am not used to being in the business I am in and growing up in the bay area.

Mi Casa

Our house is ready for demo. Sir meets me with a couple people to help him with my "bomb shelter" as we are calling it. It will be under the front yard grass and entrance will be through the coat closet in the house. The house has an accent wall that is all Kona wood. I plan to keep it but it needs a coat of oil. I am planning to tear up all the floors and have tile throughout. I originally wanted concrete but I think with all the movement of the island it will just lead to costly repairs down the road.

I picked a concrete looking tile that will be throughout the entire house. I do not want to deal with rug. I will get rugs for the rooms but I do not want anything permanent. I remember one assignment I had in Washington, the man's house was all white carpet. I think it was a popular style in the eighties. I am not sure why he never remodeled but it was a disaster to get a clean kill that night.

He was a guy that liked his women to fight back, as in his attacks where foreplay. So when I surprised him he was not too happy at first but got excited in the fact I was a female assassin. Dirty people never cease to amaze me. Anyway, instead of giving him a timely heart attack it became a game of cat and mouse. I got some good stabs in and he threw a couple punches. My bruised body was nothing in comparison to his bleeding arm and leg. When he fell down the stairs at the end blood went everywhere. I was a little stunned at what lay before me. I had never left such a gruesome scene. I made sure I left nothing of myself behind and was back home to heal before his body was found. His personal chef found him the following afternoon when he arrived for his weekly meal prep.

Since my mark was not a highly respected man of society they chalked it up to a business dispute. The police knew he was into something but never had enough evidence on him to make an arrest. When they found him I made sure to unlock his desk and scatter some papers so the police were able to tie him to a couple murders and missing person cases.

My bruised ribs and black eye healed fast. I was able to lay low for a week after to not raise any suspicion. After that night I redid the floors in my loft in the city, the floors at my office then the floors at home. Never again will I have carpet.

My kitchen design is simple. I will do concrete counter tops with a simple white subway tile back splash and stainless steel appliances. I decided on a black bottom and white uppers for the cabinets. That way we can have any color towels and or decorations we want to spice it up.

With the dark Kona wood wall in the living room I opted for an emerald green paint. In both the guest bathrooms I am going with white wallpaper with big green palm leaves on it. With a white finishes it will tie the house together.

I have always been in love with the romantic old French style in New Orleans, the dark rich colors and dramatic accents. Since I have a fairly simple bedspread and it is crème I found a beautiful black wallpaper with a floral design to go behind our bed in the master bedroom. I will accent the room with caramel color leather sitting chairs to give it a more masculine feel. Our bathroom will be black and white tiles with gold accents and colorful towels.

I am fairly confident Eric is going to love what I am doing to the house. My idea was not to change it much but then I figured if it was going to be our forever home I wanted to make it everything I ever wanted. The guest rooms are simple, gray walls and Kona wood closet doors. The house came with plantation shutters, which I love. I am thankful the previous owners had good taste so I am not ripping much out.

The house is yellow and I am going to repaint it a teal blue with white trim. Eric loved one of the old plantation homes we saw and it was teal. I hope he likes it. I have to buy all new furniture because Eric does not have much. All I am bringing over is his desk, which is beautiful and his clothes. Since it is a four bedroom house we decided that one of the rooms be our office, weapon storage. I have a safe coming that Sir will help me place in the closet. In the office we will put up pictures and awards we have earned. Me nothing special but he has some Military stuff that will be cool to display. I want to paint the office a deep navy blue but am on the fence if it will be too much.

My patio furniture is ordered and the floors are being laid when Eric calls me for an update.

Eric: "How are things going?"

Me with a big smile: "Super."

Eric: "Are you going to tell me what is going on?"

Me: "No."

Eric: "So where are you these days?"

Me: "I'm in Hawaii."

This gets a big smile out of Eric. I am outside so I am sure he sees the palm tress in the background on our Facetime.

Eric: "Are you moving?"

Me: "I guess you could say that. I have to do a few more things before the transition is complete. And Hawaii wont be home until you are here."

Eric: "Oh, do I miss you. I can't lie to you but the Kid gave me some clues on accident. Elle told him there is a bit of construction going on near by."

Me: "Just a little."

Eric: "Did you get a total gut?"

Me: "No I am just making sure it is everything I want."

Eric: "God, how much is that going to cost?"

Me: "Nothing for you to worry about. You just need to get home safe."

Eric: "I don't even know where my home is."

Me: "Soon enough."

Eric: "You really are not going to tell me anything are you?"

Me: "Think of it like one of the HGTV shows."

Eric: "I hate those shows."

Me: "Well I guess your going to have to think of a way to get home sooner then."

Eric: " I think we will be home for Christmas. May be we an have Christmas at our house?"

Me: "I know what you are trying to do."

Eric: "Can I make one request?"

Me: "You can make as many as you want. What's up?"

Eric: "I know it may sound funny, I love your comforter set but can we get a canopy bed? I feel like it is a must in Hawaii."

Me: "Yes I love it. Anything else?"

I could tell he had more to say and wasn't saying it.

Eric: "You never told me what I owe for the house. How can I contribute?"

Me: "Your design ideas are great. You will see you have had more leverage than you think. As for the cost, you pay for our first vacation together. You still want to go to Tahiti?"

Eric: "I feel like I am getting off easy here."

Me: "Better make it a bungalow over the water."

Eric: "Deal"

Eric did express he wanted an actually garage not a carport. The house already had a two-car garage but I made sure to bring it up to my level. I am having the floor coated; the walls put up and painted. I am also putting in storage along with a work-bench and a shoe wall. Since we both agreed we do not want to wear shoes in the house I found this shelving until that goes on the wall to hang shoes. With all the bugs here I do not want any surprised when putting on my shoes.

Off to the Fog

With my dad in full construction mode I decided to head back to the bay and take care of some things. Danielle for one was devastated I was moving. We have always been near each other. Even in college when we were apart we always met up for Holidays and Giants games. This was going to be no different but she was overly emotional about it. She seems to forget Eric won't be back until the holidays.

Summer in Half Moon Bay is the same as any other day. The only true days of summer we get seem to be in October. Funny enough when I land there are clear skies. I meet Danielle at Mezza Luna and we talk about what's new. I guess Matt has finally finished the bathrooms in their house. She is really excited about decorating.

She knows I make good money and is excited to hear about the new house. Her style is one hundred percent Joanna Gains so when I tell her about colors and show her pictures she does not know how to respond. I like the rustic furniture like her just with bold colors.

When I get home after dinner I realize this will not be my home for much longer. I am okay with it. I was raised here and am ready for taking the next step in my life. I am taking this head on and loving every second.

I wait until morning to pack up. I have more boxes than I realize. I figure I will mail them out when I get back from my assignment. Its not like I need the money but I want a distraction. I have been so focused on the house that when we got to the point in construction where I am not needed I found myself getting restless.

My work will be here in the bay. Sadly there are more criminals that come through hear than I would like to admit. San Francisco has become a hub of homeless and filth. It was once a clean thriving city now it is jam packed with selfish people. Hopefully one day it will be restored to its once glory.

I work during the day in the city. Because of the influx in crime, no one notices anything during the day any more. People are always dying on the beach from an over dose, drunkenness or some other element.

There are a lot of pockets in the city that people do not know about either, gardens that are great hiding places for bodies, dark corners and hidden nooks. People walk in and never walk out. I feel like I am cleaning house before departure. It is soothing. Plus I am a little over budget on the house and the extra money makes me feel less guilty about some of the add-ons.

I hit San Jose for a couple days and Oakland as well. These are similar areas where people can easily go missing. Thankfully Half Moon Bay is secluded enough nothing major ever happens. There are also too many town gossips to ever allow for anything to go unnoticed. I think that is why crime has stayed away, that or my father, who knows.

Danielle and I hit a couple Giants games while they are in town. I really can't wait until I can bring Eric. With me moving, Danielle and I made a deal that when I am away she gets both tickets and when I am in town I get first right of refusal. It is serious business when it comes to the Giants.

These last couple weeks have felt good to get out and get some work down. I have chosen to be more intimate with these, hand to hand and up close and personal. Is helps sharpen my skills and keep me focused. Plus, in the city every space is occupied so a sniper perch really does not make sense.

I look forward to hearing from Eric. I feel like it has been a while. We do not get to talk much. Some times we can schedule time out but it does not always fall into place. Last time I spoke to him the guys where just doing ground work. Nothing dangerous. It was nice to know that he was safe being that I was not close to help him.

I think the guys were a little sad they had not heard from Angel on this mission but since they are not in harms way there is no reason to bring her out. I fell like I need to only use her when I need her. I do not want them to rely on her that they do not do their job the way they know how.

When I was done with work I hung out with Danielle. I stayed in Half Moon Bay a couple more days before heading back to Hawaii. I know my house was still in the middle of construction but I wanted to get back and feel useful. Plus I enjoyed hanging out with Elle. Her and

I have become good friends. We have a lot in common being that the men we love are not home.

At the airport waiting for my flight to board I finally got a call from Eric.

Eric: "Hey baby cakes."

Me laughing: "Nice. It has already been forever. How are things?"

Eric: "We are just doing our duty. Mostly playing a lot of cards."

Me: "Want me to send you a care package?"

Eric: "Not unless its you."

Me: "I will be staying with Elle and the girls for a week while they finish some things at the house so you can reach me there if it is easier."

Eric: "I know the Kid is grateful you and Elle have been spending time together. I know it helps her a lot."

Me: "I am glad to do it. Her and I have become good friends."

Eric: "That means a lot to me."

Me: "I heard from my dad you called him. Anything I should know?"

Eric: "No, unless you want to tell me about the house."

Me: "Fair enough."

Eric: "Man I really want to know what is going on."

Me: "Fine I will tell you."

Eric: "Really?"

Me: "The kitchen is getting a full gut and overhaul. All the floors have been replaced and I painted."

Eric: "Thanks; that explains it all. I have no idea what house you even picked."

Me: "We will have an office."

Eric: "Thanks a lot."

Me: "Just promise me will stay in Hawaii for a while. I am making this special for us."

Eric: "Promise. I love Hawaii."

Staying with Elle and the girls is easy. I sleep in the extra room. I do not mind sharing the girl's bathroom because they do not know how to use it yet. I really do not know how Elle keeps such a clean house. She works four days a week and has two little humans that need one hundred percent of her attention.

I help make dinner while I am there to earn my keep. I think Elle likes having another adult around. She makes all the girls food so it is the least I can do to make one meal a day.

Babysitter

The morning started off like any other. I woke up, got dressed and made my way into the kitchen to get some coffee. Walking into the living room I found Elle in full panic. She was pacing back and fourth scrolling through her phone.

Me: "Hey Elle, what's up?"

Elle: "My nanny is in the hospital and have no one to watch the girls?"

Me: "Is she okay? Oh my God."

Elle: "I am in no position to miss work. I do not have anyone to watch them and do not know what to do. Deep breath, and I will figure this out."

Me: "Sorry, I don't know how to help."

Elle as the light in her head turns on: "Could you watch the girls?"

Me scared out of my mind: "Me?"

Elle: "Yeah you are great with the girls. They love you."

Me: "I have to tell you I have no idea how to take care of kids. I wasn't even a baby sitter growing up."

Elle: "I have seen you with the girls are you are perfect. Plus if you and Eric get married anytime soon, babies are sure to follow."

Me scared out of my mind still: "I can try but I really don't feel good about this."

Elle: "All you have to do is keep them alive."

And with that Elle was out the door to work. Honestly I really had nothing to worry about. I could do a ten-hour baby-sitting shift. I have tracked down and killed scarier things before. My small bit of confidence was soon destroyed when baby Katie started to cry.

I went into the master bedroom and picked her up out of her crib. She was still not having it. I checked her diaper and realized she needed to be changed. Still after getting cleaned up and changed she was not happy. I decided to see if she was hungry, she was not. Nothing I did was working. By this time her crying had woken up Simone and Simone was ready for a diaper change and breakfast.

After surviving the second diaper change and feeding Simone breakfast, Katie stopped crying when I put her on the carpet in the living room and their wiener dog Buster started to lick her. As odd as it was I went with it. Thinking I accomplished a lot I was sad to learn I only survived forty-five minuets of the morning.

I was not really prepared for anything so after breakfast I took the girls outside to play. Katie liked rolling around on the grass and Simone did her own thing. I found a couple tubes of bubbles and that was truly a life-saver. Besides the fact I got light headed the bubbles seemed to be a great entertainer. We were in the back yard two hours before the crying started again.

So per my newly founded routine I check diapers then made food. This process lasted the entire day off and on. Diaper change, food, and play. Around one in the afternoon Katie would not stop crying and I was getting worried. I really was at a loss when Simone in her cute little voice said "car ride?."

At this point I really did not know what that meant to the girls but since Elle left me the van I loaded the girls up and we took off. Katie stopped crying after the second block and they both passed out around block four. Too scared to stop driving I went to the gas station to fill up then over to the drive through shaved ice stand.

I swung by my house to see the progress and see my dad. I am sure he would have some insight for me in regards to the girls. Sir met me in the driveway wondering who I was at first. When he saw me he started to laugh.

Sir: "Look at you. What is going on?"

Me: "Elle was in a pinch so, here I am."

Sir: "Do you even know what you are doing?"

Me: "No, but does any new parent know?"

Sir: "Car rides are a great way to get them to pass out. How are you going to get them back in the house asleep?"

Me: "My plan was to just drive around until they wake up."

Sir after a big laugh: "Good luck with that. Have you driven the island already?"

Me: "Funny dad. What's going on here?"

Sir: "Flooring done, cabinets done, counter tops done, paint done. We are finishing up with the bathrooms before wall-paper. I am also going to have it cleaned before you start moving in. We have made such a mess. Also, notice the grass is back. The bomb shelter is in and settled. The door through the closet was the hardest. I do not know why you couldn't have just put it under the porch."

Me: "Oh so people could see me go in and out all the time?"

Sir: "Anyway, we should be done in another two weeks. Right around Halloween."

Me: "Perfect. Then I can start buying furniture."

Sir: "Are you getting all new stuff? Do you know what Eric wants?"

Me: "Yes I do. He gives me confirmation on our video chats. I am sure he will love it no matter what."

Sir: "Remember this is his home too. You have to take his wants into consideration."

Me: "I have been. I have picked a lot of the things he wanted."

Sir: "Okay just making sure."

Me: "Well if you need me I may be half way to Pearl City but I will be back around when they wake up."

Sir: "Good luck. You should be fine."

I drove around for another hour before Simone woke up. I treated her to a Starbucks to keep her quiet until we got back home. I managed to get Katie in the house and set up a little bed/ compound on the living room carpet. Buster laid next to her while Simone and I colored in the kitchen.

I never realized how calming coloring is. I think we colored for at least an hour until Katie woke up ready for a diaper change, food and to play. We were outside playing with the bubbles when Eric called for our weekly video chat.

Eric: "What on earth are you doing?"

Me: "I am blowing bubbles until I pass out."

Eric: "Why?"

Me: "Because today I am watching the girls all on my own. I am helping Elle out."

Eric: "Oh, My, God. No way."

Me: "Yeah I am! What's the big deal?"

Eric: "Wow, I just never."

Me: "Never what?"

Eric: "Don't get me wrong you are great with them when we go over there but I figured it wasn't your thing."

Me: "But I told you I wanted kids one day. What are you getting at?"

Eric: "I know I just didn't think you were ready for them quite yet that's all. Really. No insult in that."

Me: "Well it is harder than I thought. But I have managed to keep them alive this long."

Eric: "What have you been doing?"

Me: "Diaper changing, feeding them and playing. We did bubbles earlier before we went on a two and a half hour car ride in which they both took a nap. Simone and I colored for an hour and now bubbles again."

Eric: "You colored?"

Me: "Yes, it was actually quite relaxing. I will be sending you one in your next care package."

Eric: "Funny."

Me: "Ill send one to everyone then. Just you see."

It was kind of a shot to my ego Eric did not think I was capable or able to handle kids. I guess he really did not know how fierce I was so I am not going to be offended. Though my dad did not really have much faith in me either. I really hope if I have kids some day I am better. Today wasn't entirely hard.

We were still outside playing when Elle got home. She was so happy to see the girls and they were all smiles to see her. It was sweet to witness. I told Elle our day and she was surprised I treated Simone to Starbucks. I felt guilty before she told me I didn't have to do it.

Me: "It was my pleasure. I needed an afternoon coffee and I wanted to make sure she was quiet and did not wake up Katie."

Elle: "That was sweet of you to do that."

Me: "I feel like it was for my benefit. I did what ever it took."

Elle with a laugh: "That's the only way."

The rest of the evening was quiet. We ate dinner and went to bed. I really did not realize how tired I was until I woke up the next morning and found myself passed out in bed with all the lights on and my open book by my side. I guess I hit the bed and was out immediately.

Kids take a lot of you mentally and physically. I was sore the next day. My arms were feeling it. I know I held both the girls a lot but it did not seem too bad. I am in for a big change in my life when Eric and I decide to have children. I think two is manageable. I do not think I would have been so good with another one added in the mix.

All Hallows Eve

Not realizing it but Halloween was around the corner. I decided to hang out with Elle and the girls for a bit then head back to the mainland to spend one last holiday with Danielle. I wanted to get some work out of the way before Eric came home. I promised myself when he got back I would go down to just the Marketing stuff and spend as much time with Eric as possible.

I also want to spend some time with Danielle being I may not be back for Thanksgiving. Since Eric has been gone I have been floating through life. Making it up as I go. Now that he was coming home I got into focus mode and started planning.

After a couple days with Danielle I went to Seattle to meet a marketing client and clean up a few things as well. Over the years I have come up with whimsical terms for what I do. Clean the streets, charity work, fixing society. At first I thought it was to make myself feel better but I think it just helps me cope, humor is always a cure.

Back in the Bay I get the office in order. I feel like I keep doing it but each time I do it better. I get some clothes I know I am going to want and take them to the post office to ship. I also get online and make some furniture purchases of things I know I cannot get on the island.

The new house already had plantation shutters when I bought it so I do not need any window coverings even though Pottery Barn has some I really like. I figure since we are starting fresh together and neither of us has any dishware I hit up Williams and Sonoma. The nice thing is I can have it all shipped there and or picked up in the store.

Once I get back I have to go get a vehicle. Eric has a motorcycle and I am not going to bring my mustang. I was thinking of a Jeep Wrangler. I have been renting them lately and I like them. These seem fun and I like how easy they are to park. Eric mentioned a Toyota Tacoma. I will do some research. I guess it wont hurt to test drive and see what Hawaii has.

I have some work to do in San Jose so I take care of it fast and decide to hit Stevens Creek Boulevard and test-drive some vehicles. Since I just had time to kill I test drive some SUV's too. I really like the Audi Q7. I know that is a total mom car but it is nice to know what is in store for me down the road. The BMW M5 is so much fun too. I really do not need anything that fast and I do not need to draw attention to myself.

On my way home I stop at Standford Shopping Center to pick up a couple more things when I happen to see a man in the parking garage that is not looking for his car. I have seen him walking up and down the isles for a while now just scanning the area. I figure I will play dumb and see what happens.

He notices me when I get out of my car and starts to follow me. I pretend that I forgot something in my car and head back to my parking spot. As I am positioned in between a Denali and a Mini Van I make sure there is enough room around all vehicles for me to maneuver. As I start to lock up my car I see a black van driving slowly in my direction. Since it passes some empty spots I know it is connected to my wandering guy.

The guy comes up to me and asks me for change as the van door opens and two other men hop out. In any other circumstance I should be a terrified young woman about to be abducted. But they have no idea who they are trying to take. I play coy and act the part. The guys get me in the van and take off in a hurry. As we get out of the mall parking lot I make my move. I take out the two guys in the back with me. They had no idea what hit them. The passenger gets a knife to the throat and as I slowly pull it out the driver starts to freak out. He reaches to make a call and I toss the phone in the back with the two dead bodies.

I instruct the drive to a place I know will be empty. This time of day there will be no witnesses. He starts to cuss me out as we park. Telling me I don't know who I am messing with blab blab blab. When he least expects it I slit his throat. I toss his body in the back with the others and get myself cleaned up. Thankfully I have a big hooded sweatshirt on and when I pull it off I realize that is all that is dirty. I toss it in the back of the van and pour out the liter of Jim Beam they have laying around. I lite a match and let the van burn.

I walk a way down the road where there is a college apartment complex and order an Uber. As I get back to the mall I use the rest room to clean my hands and knife. I text my dad the code for an unexpected detour, as we call it, all in code and he responds with a thumbs up.

Back at the mall I go to the Stanford shop to get a new sweatshirt. I really will not be needing one in Hawaii but I am cold now and want to be comfortable being it is an outside mall.

My encounter makes me think of how many women have gone missing from this mall. Where the guys amateurs or a part of something bigger? I saved the drivers phone to send to Sir for information. Just to be on the safe side. I am all of a sudden sad for all the women that this takes by surprise; that are too busy on their cell phones or clueless about the dangers and allow themselves to be caught in these situations. I am also sad for all the women that prepare but are still over powered and never recover. I bet I am one in a million that is capable of handling the situation the way I did. I feel like that is a statistic I am not okay with.

High School should have required self-defense as a mandatory class in P.E. I feel if we were all prepared and capable it might deter some of these savages from kidnapping women and children for profit and pleasure. I remember my old Karate teacher and how he would lecture us about respect, self esteem, confidence and the ways of the world. In stead of P.E. mandatory karate would not only prepare people for dangers but it may deter them from getting into trouble in the first place. Karate helps children and adults improve discipline and mental toughness, which these days everyone acts like whinny brats. Karate is good for stress management, endorphins and overall mood. So many more people would smile in life if it was taught in school along with cooking, checks and balance and basic life skills. If only.

The rest of my trip home I get my mail organized so I can make one more trip to Chicago. Eric and I spoke earlier and he is overly excited to come home. I sent all the guys a care package of Cheetos, a multipack of candy from Costco and some crossword puzzles. I know it is super lame but it is something special they cannot get there.

When Eric gets home I have already decided that I am going to cook him his favorite meal. He loves his mother's lasagna and she sent me the recipe. I am going to make her garlic bread as well. I have made it for Elle and the girls a couple times for practice. When it comes to traditional cooking I am okay but these true, good, classic all day recipes I need to work on. I have only ever had to worry about myself. I am happy to report that I can now feed a small army with minimal effort.

For Halloween I hang out with Danielle and Matt. We dress up and hand out candy at their house. There have always been families in their neighborhood so it is a good place to trick-o-treat. Danielle and Matt dress up as Professor McGonagall and Professor Snape from Harry Potter and I go as a Black Cat. Danielle had food delivered and we took turns answering the door. I know they have never thought of me as the third wheel, as just apart of the equation but I think they are really going to miss having me around.

I called it an early night, ten thirty which is really not at all but there were no more kids coming to the door and I knew I had a lot more to do before the official move, in two days. Two more days and I was officially a Hawaiian. I was going to miss Half Moon Bay, it has been home my whole life. This new adventure with Eric was the first of so many things. The new chapter was beginning.

Dad

Arriving in Hawaii, Sir picks me up and we head straight for the house. En route he goes over some new findings in regards to our Mystery Man. He has been doing research in his down time and came across two possible men that could be our guy.

Suspect number one is a Russian born man, mixed parents that where killed in the late sixties. He has been an up and comer in the crime world with connections in drugs, guns and human trafficking. He started off as an errand boy for a war criminal while still in an orphanage and learned the ropes really young. Since then he has replaced his mentor and expanded the business. He is known as a brutal, soulless man that has no emotion when in human-to-human situations. He has a great poker face and seems like money is the force behind his success. Though greed seems like the likely motivator Sir thinks the rise to power gives him access to avenge his parent's deaths.

Sir's research on number one's parents revile they were both evolved with his mentor. Apparently the student surpassed the teacher when he shot him point blank one night and announced his take over. Even though he took out his parent's boss he still feels the Americans should pay for their deaths. There were a group of tourist and marines in the area round the time of his parents murders and he is trying to track down the Americans identities to apply blame to the murders. The man cannot accept that his parents worked for a bad guy doing bad things and has to put blame on someone. Americans have always been an easy scapegoat, so why not?

Sir found out that the murder of his parents was not a hit from our organization. He seems to think it may have been a deal gone wrong or one of the many people that the boss had bad blood with.

As for suspect number two, he is a Japanese born Indian. His parents migrated for work and though his parents where from India there is no trace of them before they moved to India in 1968. After they arrived in Japan in 1974 they started to work for a wealthy family as household servants. Number two's mother was the maid and his father was the gardener.

Growing up on the families large estate number two became obsessed with the life style of the homeowners. They had three daughters around his age and he immediately made friends with all of them. As he got older he started to make connections outside the estate which lead him into a life of back door deals and smuggling. When he ran into one of the daughters one night in college it went from good to bad in a heart beat.

He was so submerged in his shady dealings that he lead the girl into the arms of one of his partners that tried to take advantage of the young girl. When he made the move to help her, his colleagues turned against him and he was forced back to the estate, ultimately hiding out. This made him so upset that he finally left the estate to confront the people that tried to hurt the young girl.

When he met up with them it turned into a blood bath. He and another young man where the only survivors though it left him with a limp and the other young man blind in one eye. From that moment on he was a force to be reckoned with. Rumors spread about the two men; which made them jump to the top of the food change fast.

He was then married to the young woman and with her families money and his income of odd jobs he started to live the life he always wanted. The group of men he fought that gruesome night where all gathered for an exchange involving guns. Two of the men happened to be ex marines from America. He thinks the marines had something to do with him being ousted in the first place and their presence caused the fight.

Number two seems far-fetched but since his rise to power our organization has taken out many of his men. We have taken out his clients, his friends and his cousin in which he was really close too. His dealings have put him on our watch list but he has backing from an unknown source we have been trying to uncover for a while now. Taking him out will only kill any progress we have made.

Something about both men did not sit well with me. I did not think either men were who we are looking for. I think it is someone that has been sitting back and lurking in the shadows. It is only until recently that he has chosen to be known. I do not necessarily think they are looking for revenge on my marines but rather smoke out one of my own. I have a feeling we are not any closer to the answer. Sir understands my concern and makes a note of it. He is going to follow up on both accounts as we see everything through. No assumptions. Facts are important and necessary. Because we take life does not mean we do not value it. We do not just kill the bad guys. We have just backing to our conclusions. It may not be the right way but is the only way we know how.

Once the final touches on the bomb shelter is complete Sir takes off to Japan to track down some more information. I think we have been given these two suspects as a front for who is really looking for us.

With Sir gone and my house complete I start ordering more items for the house and I start to decorate. Elle comes buy with the girls one night for dinner and they love it. Being that it is empty they have a blast running all around. My bed is the only furniture that has been delivered so I really just hang out in our room.

As stuff starts to arrive I place it where I imagine it would be best suited for the room. As more and more come's I make some changes. I am so consumed with it being perfect I do not realize how much time has passed. Eric will be home soon.

Turkey

oday Eric gets home and I bought the perfect welcome home dress. It is a white lace dress in the fifties house wife style. I wear my hair half up with a flower in my ear. I meet Elle at the gate and we are escorted down to the runway to meet the guys. It is exactly what you see on TV. Dad's girl is here too. I do not know her name but she is cute and I know it will mean the world to him that she came.

Madison and Boomers mom arrived together along with a couple other women I do not know. Even though we do not know each other's names we all know each other. We are strong women that are waiting for the loves in our life to arrive home safely. It is a bond that no one else could understand.

Three men I do not know exit the plane. Then Boomer, Doc, the Kid, Dad and Eric. Of course he is last, last of the group I know. When he sees me we run toward each other. I jump into his arms and we hug for a long time. I have missed him so much and I know by the kiss he gives me he missed me just as much. Every thing is okay with the world at this moment in time.

In all the commotion we go around and give hugs to every one then head to the car. I have yet to decide on a vehicle so I rented a Jeep wrangler in the meantime. Eric can't keep his hands off me and I love it. When we make it to the car there is a pause. So much time has passed but everything is exactly how we left it. I know for some families the case is not the same. I am fortunate. But with what Eric has already experienced and what I have been exposed too I truly believe we could conquer anything together.

Eric is quiet during our drive home. I start to get nervous because I really want him to like it. I am all for making changes if he wants but I just want it to be perfect for him. As we pull into our new drive way I see a smile play across his face. I park in the driveway so we can enter the front door.

Before entering Eric grabs my arm and pulls me back. He picks me up into his arms.

Eric: "I have to carry you over the threshold the first time. Makes it legit."

I do not argue. When we get inside he sets me down and looks around. He is all smiles as I take his hand and move him from room to room. Before we head to the bedroom I take him on the patio.

Eric: "I love it."

Me: "You haven't even seen the most important room yet."

Eric: "Doesn't matter. I know I am going to love it. Its home."

Me: "I was hoping you would say that."

Eric: " It is perfect. You made it a combination of both of us. Show me the bedroom."

We head to the room and he smiles. I know he loves it but his silence is making me a little crazy. I think being away was harder than I thought. He hugs me for a long time then heads to take a shower. I know he showers after long trips to unwind so I leave him to relax as I make some lunch.

When he comes into the kitchen I can tell he is better. He is wearing the board shorts I bought him and put in his dresser. I take it he has been investigating.

Me: "Tell me. What do you like, dislike. Lay it on me."

Eric: "I actually like it all."

Me: "Really, you don't sound too confident."

Eric: "Well when you were having me pick colors and tiles I really had no idea what I was going to come home to, but this is great. I love the office and our bedroom is perfect. I could stay in there forever."

Me: "I knew you would like it. I was hesitant on the kitchen and paint colors."

Eric: "I love the outside color but I know why you picked it. You also picked a house with all our wants."

Me: "I did my best."

Eric roamed around the house the rest of the day. He would make comments about different things. He loved the couch I picked out and printed black and white photos of our vacation and time together as the artwork around the house. As he was taking it all in I really was hoping he didn't ask what everything cost. I do not want him to worry or be concerned with that.

The following day we did the same thing; a lot of nothing. We lounged around, went into the pool and walked over to the beach. Eric did laundry and organized his office how he liked it. He even cleaned up the safe and organized the weapons.

It was nice settling in and being home together. The guys were set to go to Ululani's in a couple of days. I know this has become an important ritual of theirs. I am glad they have something that helps them heal. It is something they do that helps them move back into a daily routine here.

Eric: "We should have Christmas here."

Me: "Yes, every year."

Eric: "No, I mean host Christmas here this year. With the guys and their families."

Me: "I like that idea."

Eric: "Ill let the guys know."

After the guys got back from Maui, things fell into routine. Eric would come home and do something in the garage or outside before coming in for dinner. We spent a lot of time I the back yard. One afternoon Eric went looking for something. I really had no idea so I went on with my computer work until he started to call for me.

Eric in a hard tone: "Will you come here please?"

Me: "Eric, what is it?"

Eric: "What is this?"

Eric found my bug out bag. It was filled with extra clothes, toiletries, a couple blades, two guns, ammo and a first aid kit. The bag was not very big but filled with things I would need in case of an emergency.

Me: "That is my bug out bag."

Eric: "Why would you need one of these?"

Me: "I have just always had one. In case of a natural disaster."

Eric: "Not incase you needed to slip out in the middle of the night and disappear?"

Me: "Why would I do that?"

Eric: "I don't know. Why would you need a bug out bag?"

Me: "I told you I had one back in Half Moon Bay. It is something both my sisters have and something my dad has always told us to have on hand. You do remember who my dad is right?"

Eric: "Sorry. I was not expecting this."

Me pulling out the second bag: "I made you one too."

Eric after a light laugh: "No way. I just think I'm not one hundred percent yet. I don't want you to think anything between us has changed. I just am off. I'm sorry for freaking out about this."

Me: "No worries. I remember my dad needed some down time when he got home from his trips. I get it."

Eric: "You really do. Sorry I am being weird."

Me: "You are not weird. It's a process we need to get though together."

Eric: "You promise?"

Me: "I moved in with you."

I know that Marines and other service men and women sometimes have issues readjusting to society when they have been gone for long periods of times. I know when I went for my summer holiday mission I had a hard time going to class afterwards. Since the guys did not see any violence while they were away some think it should be easy for them to jump right back in to day-to-day stuff. But being away form their loved one and home is still hard on them. It would be hard on anyone. This mission still didn't change the fact that they all intentionally put their lives at risk for others. There has to be times when they question themselves. There is an internal struggle that I can only touch on and relate too. I wish I knew how to help.

Seeing Eric working through it and trying to adjust after being away and coming home to a new home, I feel like may be I should feel the same. Since I have traveled the world, killed many I have never had a problem coming home and going right back to normal. I wonder if there is something wrong with me that I should seek help for. Sir always said I adjusted well. Like I have an on and off switch. I hope that turns out to be an okay issue.

After visiting Maui, Eric invited the guys and their families over for a Barbeque. We always have them at the Kids house and I think Elle is glad for the change. No clean up. I set up the dinning table outside and Eric is on the grill. I think this is what he needed to break in the new house. With kids running around and people everywhere I hang out in the kitchen getting the food ready.

We decided to do ugly steaks with hot dogs for the kids. I slice pineapple because what is a Hawaiian Barbeque without grilled pineapple. I set everything out on the island. Guacamole, chips, salsa, beans, veggies, ranch dip and fruit. It felt good to have people over and to be entertaining. It is something I have never done in the past. I have never had a reason too or someone to do it with.

Our little event is nice. Even though we had a mess to clean up we left it for the morning. That night I think Eric was able to fully heal from being away. We melted into each other and all was right with the world.

Eric: "Thank you for giving me a home."

Me: "I am happy for this adventure with you."

As we settle into living together in our new home I am sad we have to leave. I know we promised his mother and father we would go see them for Thanksgiving but I did not want this to end. Now that it was all real and happening I was scared for it to end.

Our Thanksgiving trip went fast and we were glad to be back home. Eric's parents were delighted we moved in together and are going to try and come out for Christmas. Being on the mainland we also got some holiday shopping in. Eric's mom loves Black Friday shopping so for the first time in my life I went with her to a few spots and we were able to snag some good deals. I do not know if I would ever try it again but it was a fun experience.

Coming home this time Eric again had to carry me over the threshold.

Me: "Why do you insist on doing this?"

Eric: "Because it makes me feel good. And since we are not married I feel like it is the right thing to do since we are living in sin."

Me: "Oh, when did you start getting so old fashion?"

Eric: "Not old fashion, just want to do right by you."

Me: "Ok, Ill go along with it."

With Eric being home I have not been on a mission in a while but still had to attend to my Marketing duties. It was easy to do from home. I missed the work. I did not want to leave now that Eric was home but I sensed a calling. I had a duty that I was neglecting. I wanted to have my cake and eat it too. It was time for me to figure out how to work and be with Eric.

He knows I travel for work but he does not know how much I actually travel. I would have to set up a schedule for myself and allow myself to leave occasionally. May be start with once a quarter and hit it hard when he gets sent away.

For now Eric and I needed to look for a permanent vehicle and start shopping for Christmas decorations. That is one thing I did not think of when getting the house ready for his return.

Mele Kalikimaka

We went to a couple dealerships before making our way Kaimuki Toyota. Eric liked the Jeep Cherokee but did not like the way it drove, and the Wrangler was not enough of a vehicle in case we had family in town. Once I mentioned getting a Tacoma it was like he did not want to see anything else.

So we agreed on a charcoal gray four door Tacoma with cloth enterer. We got the upgraded model and Eric was pumped to finally drive it off the lot. I was thankful that was over. The back and forth with the salesman was exhausting. I do not see how people have the time to waste a whole day buying a car. We ended up buying it outright with the money Eric's parents gave us as a house-warming gift. His mom agreed that we could not keep renting and a motorcycle can't be used to go grocery shopping.

As if we were not exhausted enough we decided to hit Home Depot for some decorations. We got a pre-light tree and enough lights to light the entire block. I think Eric is going for a National Lampoons vibe this year.

We pulled into the garage and left everything in the back and went inside. We were about to call it a day when I found a little blue box on the kitchen counter.

Eric: "I missed our one year anniversary. You did not say anything but I want you to know I didn't forget. I am sorry I couldn't be here to celebrate it with you."

Me totally off guard: "I really didn't expect this."

Eric: "I want you to know next year will be better."

Me: "This is perfect. I don't need anything else but you."

Eric is really a romantic at heart. He said our anniversary date is the day we met at Ululani's. I was moved that he cared so much. He got me a simple pearl bracelet from Tiffany's. It was significant to us moving to Hawaii. I really felt bad I did not remember and or think to get him anything. I felt like I was the stereotypical male in this relationship.

Me: "Oh Eric, I didn't get you anything."

Eric: "Are you kidding me, look at this place. I know you put a lot more into making this our home than you would like me to believe. You have moved mountains for me. Really, your gift does not compare."

Me: "Trust me, it is more than I could have ever imagined."

Eric: "We still have a lot of decorations to buy, want to hit it hard again tomorrow?"

Me: "Yes, we are going to have the best decorations in town, and a perfect family gathering. Would you be ok if I got holiday dishes? My grandmother had some she used for Christmas only and I would like to follow in the same tradition."

Eric: "Sure."

Not really knowing what he signed on for but I placed my order that night while he was in the shower. We will have the most amazing Christmas dinner table. Thank you Pottery Barn.

We finished shopping for all the decorations so now it was time to start decorating. We started on the outside and I helped Eric get the lights up around the house and up the tree in the front of the house. We also went wild and got a blow up Santa that pops out of a chimney.

Moving inside we got the tree set up between the living room by the French doors. We hung garland over the fireplace mantel with our stockings. Eric and I picked them out at Pottery Barn. I picked out a Faux Fur one and Eric picked out the red and black plaid one. Not realizing it we only had two ornaments on the tree and we need a star or angel for the top of the tree.

Eric: "I think our work here is done."

Me: "At least for today. We still need a couple things."

Eric: "I will leave that up to you. I am pooped."

Me: "Of course. It will give me something to do while you are at work."

Eric: "What does that mean? What do you have planned?

Me: "I liked the Pottery Barn set up. What do you think of that?"

Eric: "We do not need to get too crazy."

Me: "I know, I will take it easy."

I did not go too crazy but I did get a wreath, some battery operated candles, a mercury Tree set, a bunch or ornaments that coordinated with our lives together, a table runner, tree skirt, napkins, some throw pillows and a Christmas Card holder. When Eric got home from work he did not notice my shopping spree bags all over but instead went over to the tree where I added the ornaments.

Eric: "You got ones that relate to us."

Me: "You noticed."

Eric: "Yeah, I am not totally dense. How many did you get?"

Me: "Just eight. I figured we will get more each year."

Eric: "Lets see....A heart frame with a picture of us and the year, our first year together. A heart, a starfish for Hawaii and a house for our new home together. A little red truck for our first vehicle purchase. Kissing fish, an ugly sweater and a beer mug. Cute."

Me: "I am glad you like the. I did not want to get carried away."

Eric rolling his eyes: "I am sure you showed great restraint."

Me: "You don't even know. This Christmas is going to be magical. Do you want to have people over Christmas Eve or Christmas Day?"

Eric: "My mom called and said they are going to come through Christmas Day. I think they are leaving Christmas Day to fly to my Aunts. So lets do Christmas Eve."

Me: "Perfect. I will get the invitations sent ASAP."

Eric: "Oh wow, Invitations. They guys are going to give me crap for this."

Me: "Stop, Elle and I agreed we are going to do a white elephant gift game for the adults and Danielle suggested Santa come for the kids earlier. Elle liked it but I think it might be too much."

Eric: "Wow, you are really going all out."

Me: "I just want it to be perfect."

Eric: "I will be perfect as long as we are together, nothing else matters."

Me: "You are too sweet."

Christmas Eve was perfect. I got Eric and I matching Hawaiian Christmas Print outfits. He wore his button up with some jeans and I accessorized my dress with all Eric's beautiful gifts. Eric greeted everyone as they came in. I had a popcorn ball bowl set out on the back yard kitchen table with bowls of mixed nuts.

On our kitchen table I had food set out for everyone to eat as they got hungry. I had black and green olives, chicken wings, jalapeno poppers, crab dip, onion dip, cookies that Eric and I made and decorated ourselves, fudge, pumpkin pie, apple crisp pie, turkey, stuffing, mash potatoes, gravy, fresh rolls and a salad.

In the kitchen I had a hot coco, eggnog and hot cider station set up. We had other drinks at the outdoor kitchen. Eric, his parents and I cooked all day on the food and everything was perfect. The food was delicious and I made sure I ate before everyone came. I was glad I did because once people started to arrive I was all over the place.

I ended up not hiring a Santa to come for the kids but made sure they had goodie bags and a present to open after everyone had a chance to eat. Our adult gift exchange was hilarious. We opted for the present pass game. Each person picks a number. You can keep the present or steal another person gift. Words where exchanged and yelling occurred but everyone was happy with what they got. No one really cared except for Eric's dad who was holding a handle of Crown Royal at the end.

The night was perfect. Everyone got along and was so happy. Eric moved around the room with ease and I could see how happy he was. We would meet up now and then for a hug and a kiss then be on our way helping someone with drinks or replenishing the food.

The kids opened gifts and ate way too many sweets. The other guests liked their party favors I made. There were a couple gift exchanges between close friends. It was a night of love and friendship. The guys shared a moment on the patio with the cigars I got them.

At the end of the night when everyone was gone we took a moment and made a plate of food and had our dinner together on the couch. We talked and laughed about the night. I was a wonderful moment. Before going to bed I hopped off the couch and grabbed a small teal box from under the tree. It was Eric's Christmas present and for once he was getting the little teal box.

Surprised and hesitant he opened it up. It was a set of silver Dog Tags with an engraving. One tag I had angel wings engraved on one side and on the other "To Always Protect you." On the other tag I had the coordinates of Ululani's engraved on one side and a heart on the other.

Eric with tears in his eyes: "Thank you."

Me: "I wasn't sure if you were going to be willing to wear two sets of Dog Tags."

Eric: "For you anything. This is so special. What to the numbers mean?"

Me: "They are the coordinates of Ululani's."

Eric with his eyes closed: "This is perfect. You are perfect."

And with that I earned myself an over the top romantic kiss. He held me for a long time after. I did not think my present was going to go over that well but I am glad it did. I wanted him to have something special to keep him safe. And with out having to tell him I was his Angel and I would always do everything in my power to keep him safe. It was my way of telling him without having to tell him. I am sure he just figured I know the importance of the Angel so that is why I included it. I felt a load off my shoulders and I am glad he loved it.

The Big Vacation

With Christmas come and gone New Years Eve was upon us. Eric was to report to San Diego for training in a few days so we opted to stay home for our first New Years Eve living together.

I made some snacks for us to munch on throughout the night. We turned on the TV to watch the ball drop and played music in the background. We danced, took turns making each other drinks and eating way more than we should. It was so much fun. We laughed at each other and when we finally took a break on the couch we were done for.

The next morning we woke up realizing we did not make it to the ball drop. We were hung over and in no mood to get off the couch. After a cleaning up and a shower we ate a late hung over brunch on the patio and decided to make it a movie marathon in bed rest of the day.

Hawaii is a blast for New Years Eve. There are fireworks and the black sky turns gray after the cloud of smoke covers the island. We missed all that because we were so involved with each other. I had bought fireworks and we did not even touch them. This was by far my favorite New Years of all time. I think things are going great between us. Eric keeps mentioning our Tahiti vacation.

With Eric going to San Diego for a couple weeks I decided to get some work of my own done. I plan to fly out the same day he left to San Francisco and take on a couple jobs. I figured I could get a lot done while he was in SoCal and then we could meet up after training was over for my birthday. I was hoping he might want to hit up Universal Studios or something fun like that. I told him I was game for anything so we will se what he has planned.

With the Holidays come and gone we finally getting settled in our new home together it was weird arriving at SFO. It was natural being here even though I did not live here anymore. I stopped by the office before I headed home, to my old home.

I could tell Sir had been there because there were some items in the refrigerator. I am thankful they were not expired yet because I had no desire to go to the grocery store for anything else. I was feeling lazy.

I checked in with Sir and got my travel arrangements made before I went to sleep. The next day I met up with Danielle and we hit the Ritz for a golf and Spa day. It was a typical misty, foggy day on the coast so golfing sucked and the spa treatments were very well received. I talked to Eric once before I started my journey. I was driving to Vegas for a couple days before hitting up Chicago for a week and then over to Europe. America was always complicated, working on your home turf seemed to pose the problem you might run into someone you may know. I try and keep tabs of everyone I went to school with so I know when I travel someone under another name that I do not run into anyone that blows my cover. Being I am easily forgotten and I have been invisible most my life it does not make it too hard to cover my tracks.

Vegas is sadly too easy. The influx of people that come to Sin City over the holidays is insane. They come to indulge all their wicked desires. Drinking and catching a show is one thing but what people do not see behind the close doors is what makes my hair stand on end.

They're where seven targets in Vegas alone. It took only two nights because no one ever sleeps. A knock at the door at three in the morning is common for the sick individuals looking for delights. My last target took longer than the rest. I sat in the bar at the Bellagio for about an hour before he left with the high priced service girl. She locked in on him as soon as he arrived and did not leave his side. I could not get close. I found her to be too aggressive for your typical prostitute.

When I went to the bar I was able to copy his key card so I will go and check on him in about twenty minuets. I figured if I caught them both in mid performance I could kill two birds with one stone. There was something off about this girl and I had a feeling I would soon find out what it was.

I made my way up to the room undetected. Vegas is very well monitored but coming here so many times before I knew where to travel. I slipped into the room and it was quiet. This sent my inner alarm on overdrive.

I made my way through the room and checked the closets. They were not there. What the hell happened? Right when I was done checking for bugs I heard the door click. They were just getting in?

They two were laughing for getting caught in the elevator. Of course they made the elevator ride eventful. As they started to pull off their clothes and making their way to the bed I struck. With a needle in each hand they had no time to react. If they felt the pinch they did not react. They continued to kiss until they both yawned and hit the bed. I waited in the shadows until I knew the process was complete.

As I checked to make sure I was successful I noticed the woman's face again. It was bugging me but she looked familiar. I checked her purse for information and scanned her fingerprints with my phone before I did a clean sweep and left.

I sent Sir my findings. Something about the woman felt familiar. She was someone I have run into before. My instructions for the job were to take out the male and his female companion. I knew of there crimes but I have never recognized someone like that before. Sometimes they were famous or well known somehow.

On my way to Chicago I got the information clarifying I knew the girl. I went to middle school with her. She was a very successful call girl in Vegas. I did not remember her at all. Apparently, she had been abused by an older boyfriend in eighth grade and her mom moved her to Vegas. Her record was a laundry list of crimes. She was apart of out target list because of the company she kept and the services she provided. She not only sold her body, but others as well. She sold drugs and weapons to bad people. No matter how many times she got caught she just kept getting in deeper. She was addicted to the lifestyle, one in which she could have avoided if her mother picked a different city.

I guess once abused something inside of her flipped. She went from all-American Athlete to Super Madam of Vegas. Some of the children she sold ended up dead, she knew it but kept on fulfilling peoples blackest desires. She went over to the dark side and there was no saving her. Once she assisted in the killing of an innocent five-year-old boy she was placed on our list for elimination.

I just do not understand people sometimes. I kill for money (and the greater good). I understand people selling themselves for issues within but why hurt innocent children? Why take away their innocents? Hurting them does not save you from what happened. It is a hard concept for me to understand. I know I will never understand why people hurt children, and I never want to. And I feel no remorse for killing the people who harm children.

Chicago was quick and easy. So many foreign transplants in Chicago this past week. With Chicago's increasing crime rate and the circle these people run in there were not many suspicions upon their deaths.

Going back to London after my last trip was healing. I really though my last trip was going to put a black cloud over London forever. Thankfully there is always a gray cloud over London so my arrival was okay.

London Royalty has always been on the target list. One falls off and another replaces it. London Royalty is much larger than people think. It is not just the Queen and Monarchy. It is a long line of men and women that have continued to carry on the radical traditions from hundreds and hundreds of years ago. People sometimes do not evolve.

With work complete I head back to meet up with Eric in Orlando. He has planned Orlando Disney World Vacation for us. I think he used my birthday to his advantage. I am totally okay with it. We are staying at Disney's Port Orleans Resort. We will be hitting up all the parks here, the Magic Kingdom, Animal Kingdom, Epcot and Hollywood Studios. I am so excited.

We meet up at the Resort and I am so excited to see Eric. We are going to have a blast. I know we plan to go to Tahiti soon but why not celebrate as much as we can together. With his schedule I want to take advantage of our time together. I guess we did not travel much when I was little and now I travel all over the world. It is just nice to finally have someone to experience life with.

We get checked and make sure we break in our room. Being away from each other for two weeks was a little more than we could handle. As we called it a night we were both excited to be big kids for the next couple of days.

We did open to close all three days. It was non-stop food and fun. Eric and I had a blast drinking around the world at Epcot but defiantly made note of the places we will not enjoy eating. We were so exhausted by the last day we barley spoke the flights home. It was enough to just lean on each other and sleep.

Getting home was welcomed. We spent a day cleaning and doing laundry. Eric had gotten a couple calls while we were in Florida and today that he had to take outside. I noticed it was the first time ever he had to take a private call. I decided to dismiss it. I am sure he would eventually tell me.

Tahiti

Over the next couple weeks we fell back into our lives. I did a lot of work from home as he went to work Monday through Friday. There were a couple days of the week when he came home later than normal yet had no explanation for it. I found it weird, was he keeping something from me? I did not have a bad feeling about it but it did not sit well with me either. When I asked him where he was I just got a general "out and about" answer.

As our trip to Tahiti was finalized, time off requests approved Eric started to act even weirder than he had been. He was still being very loving, attentive but at the same time aloof. I asked Sir about it and he offered no help. Danielle suggested I wait it our a bit and see what happens.

After all we were about to take this lavish vacation together. If there was something up I am sure he would have put a stop to our trip. Worse case scenario I could always put a tail on him and find out. Being that this is my first relationship and we are living together I wanted to act normal until I could not take it anymore.

We went over to Elle and Logan's house for a family barbeque and things were perfect. It was like nothing had been off. We were just two lovebirds enjoying life. The afternoon was wonderful. All the guys were there. Dad even brought his new girlfriend. Not new really but he was just starting to bring her around all of us. It was so funny to see how opposite they were but they worked perfectly.

Boomer: "Hey Guava, how things been?"

Me: "Same ole same ole."

Boomer: "How is married life?"

Me: "Shut up we are not married."

Boomer: "Might as well be."

Me: "I guess someday."

Boomer: "You think?"

Me: "I hope, isn't that the next step?"

Boomer: "Yes it is."

Me: "What about you? You think you will ever give a girl a chance?"

Boomer: "What makes you think I haven't already?"

Me: "Really?"

Boomer with a big laugh: "No"

Me: "Well I guess I will have to pray for you then."

Boomer: "You pray?"

Me: "Occasionally."

Boomer: "You gotta do what you gotta do."

Me: "You don't?"

Boomer: "Every day since Angel saved us."

Me: "I am glad she keeps you guys in line."

Dinner was fun. We all sat at the outside kitchen table per the norm. Food was passed around and Logan lead everyone in prayer before we ate. I was thankful for this family that welcomed me and accepted me. I was finally apart of something because of Eric and because I saved them. I will never regret my decision to help them.

Elle: "Eric's new dog tags are beautiful. What an amazing gift."

Me: "I really had a hard time figuring out what to get him. Present giving has never been my strong suit."

Elle: "It was so meaningful. You two are perfect for each other. I am glad you guys are together."

Me: "Thank you."

Hearing about Eric's gift made me think about all we have been through. No one, including him will ever know how close we really are. I know that no matter what his feelings for me are stronger than the thought of Angel. I was originally self-concise that he may never be able to commit to me for the thought he might have a chance with her someday. Then I got over myself because I know that since we are the same person that I can accept both as mine. I hope some day I can tell him about it. Some moments I am caught off guard by him, like he may already know.

We got a couple comments thrown at us about getting married. Why have we moved in together and not gotten married? I blew it off as 'one step at a time" but I noticed every time someone brought it up he got uncomfortable. I figured it was the next step in our relationship but was it? Usually these Marines married fast. It was out of the norm for a relationship to move as slow as ours. I did not know if I was reading into his behavior as something negative but I had to admit he was a little off since we got back.

Was he having second thoughts about us? Did we move in together to fast? Was I living in my own reality? Being invisible for so long may have made me socially awkward. I hope it did not damage my people skills to the point I was driving Eric away.

My paranoia did get the best of me and I checked Eric's phone records. All I found was a lot of calls to his Mother. I figured I cannot be mad at him for having a relationship with his mother. I am sure she was just consoling him on living with someone. We both had never lived with any one before so I am sure he was dealing with it the best he knows how. At that point I felt stupid for being so negative about myself. I know Eric loves me so there is no need to be adding stress to myself.

Eric: "I can't wait for our trip. I love traveling and having these experiences with you."

Me: "Same. I hope you can relax though. You have been a little tense the last couple weeks."

Eric: "I know. I am sorry. I been trying to get things done before we go so I don't have to deal with anything until I get back."

Me: "Not like they will be able to get a hold of you while we are gone. Cell reception may not be good."

Eric: "I sure hope not. I'm sorry for being all weird lately."

Me: "As long as you still love me I can deal with whatever you throw at me."

Eric: "I will always love you. That will ever change."

Me: "Good. I know living together has been an adjustment I just didn't want you to regret moving so fast with me."

Eric: "God no. I teased you about getting married last New Years Eve when we went to Vegas remember."

Me: "Yeah but I knew you were joking. Not like you were ready for that."

Eric: "I was."

Me: "You where?"

Eric: "I think I would have married you at Ululani's that day. You caught me at the right time."

Me: "Shut up, don't be stupid. You got all weird at Elle and Logan's when they were teasing us about moving in together before getting married."

Eric: "Because I felt bad. Like I did you an injustice for living in sin with you. I hope I haven't let you down."

Me: "No way. We have done it our way. Everyone can take their opinion's and shove it."

Eric: "I like the way you think. You are perfect."

Me: "Now you are being stupid."

Eric: "No I am not. I think you are perfect in every way. You are beautiful, smart, funny and I love spending time with you. I even let you decorate our home and I love it."

Me: "Okay."

Eric: "You really can't take a complement can you?"

Me: "You are the only person that has ever given them to me. It is overwhelming sometimes. I guess I have always been invisible to men, no one ever noticed me before you."

Eric with an inquisitive look: "That's not true. When we say you walk up from the beach the first time we met you we all went silent. You were a vision. Then when word got around how you could shoot. Guys on base were asking if you and I were really a couple. I had to lock it down fast before anyone else tried to move in."

All I could say after that was I love you and good night. It was a load off my mind. I think I was being mental the last couple of weeks. I know he had a life here before me. Since I really never had a life outside of work I had to find things to get involved in.

I did not pack much for our trip to Tahiti knowing we would spend most of the time in bed or in our swimsuits. We are leaving at three in the afternoon, traveling business class to Tahiti. I am thankful we upgraded because the six plus hours of sitting can get uncomfortable. Eric is not as relaxed as normal. I am not sure what is going on but he was nervous during our security check and so stiff at take off. I am hoping he chills out or this trip is going to be awful. After our talk I thought he was ok. May be he was nervous about all the special upgrades I made. Who knows at this point.

We got to Tahiti and checked into our bungalow over the water. It was picturese and no photograph could ever do it justice. Not using any logic I took Eric's hand to our balcony and pushed him over the patio's edge into the ocean. Then I jumped in after him, fully clothed. We laughed for at least ten minuets before we swam over to the latter and climbed up. We de-clothed, showered and spent the rest of the day in bed.

Dinner was wonderful. We were served on our patio. We just laughed talking about me pushing Eric in with our wet clothes still sitting in a pile on the balcony. Eric was finally starting to relaxed. It was nice to have him back to normal. We dressed the next morning for a bike ride. He took a little longer in the bathroom than normal but it is not like we had anywhere to be on time. We were on our own time, yet it still felt like something was off.

Our bike ride was a nice distraction. We checked out the island and got some snacks. When we got back to our room for lunch we changed into our swim suits before eating on the balcony. Eric was nervous again and I really was out of ideas on what to do. We ate lunch and went for a swim.

After our swim I decided to make us some drinks, hopefully mellow Eric out a bit. I poured us some stiff drinks and headed back to the patio balcony. Eric was passing back and forth.

Me: "Hey, this is vacation you need to relax."

Eric: "I am, I am having the time of my life."

Me: "Okay. If you say so."

Eric: "Really everything has been amazing."

Me: "Okay. Take a sip of this."

Eric lightened up a bit after that. We were planning to head down to dinner so I decided to jump in the shower and get ready. When I walked out of the bathroom in my sundress ready for dinner I realized right then why Eric was being so weird. Everything finally made sense.

Flower petals made a path to the bed and then to the patio balcony where a romantic dinner was set up. Eric was waiting for me already dressed in shorts and a button up shirt.

Me: "What is all this?"

Eric: "This is why I have been acting weird."

Me with a laugh: "It's beautiful but you are a decorated solider. Setting up a romantic dinner stressed you out?"

Eric got down on one knee and opening a little teal box: "No this is what I have been stressing over. Will You Marry Me?"

Printed in the United States
By Bookmasters